MUCK

AGAIN!

More Humorous Tales

From

JOYCE WILSON

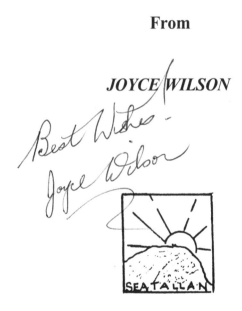

Best Wishes -
Joyce Wilson

SEATALLAN

Published by Seatallan Press
6 Downfield Lane, Bigrigg, Egremont,
Cumbria CA22 2UY

First published 2002

ISBN 0-9528919-4-8

Printed and bound in Great Britain by
Athenaeum Press Ltd; Gateshead, Tyne & Wear

Also by Joyce Wilson

'Muck But No Money' (1993)

'More Muck And Less Money' (1995)

'Even More Muck' (1997)

CONTENTS

MUCK AGAIN!

1.

A VISIT TO THE DENTIST

'Your sister always manages to arrange her visits at the busiest times of the year, why can't she come in the wintertime when it doesn't matter?' called Jackson sharply to his wife Edith as she worked in the scullery.

'But Dad,' interrupted his daughter Esther, 'you can't expect a woman in her delicate state of health to walk a mile in all weathers to visit us.'

Jackson's ears pricked up at Esther's words.

'What state of health is she in? Her husband's been dead a good few years now ... certainly more than nine months!'

Esther giggled at her father's misunderstanding.

'Don't be silly Dad, she's a town lady so we can't expect her to rough things on a dirty farm in the middle of winter!'

'Well, your mother had the same upbringing, and ever since I persuaded her to buy them new wellington boots a couple of weeks ago I can't stop her paddling about in as much muck as she can find. Unlike me Esther, you didn't see her slithering across the pig hull floor this morning, just as if she was performing on a skating rink! The old sow had a job to catch up with her breakfast ... she almost lost it to them two young shotts who reached the trough well ahead of her.'

He shook his head sadly.

'Old age comes to all of us ... except your mother of course ... she got a new lease of life the very minute she put on them silent sneaking boots. But I'm not so sure that it was such a good idea of mine to persuade her to buy them.'

'She paid for them out of her egg money!' pointed out Esther tartly.

'That's just why a farmer gives little job like that to his womenfolk, it lets them buy a few luxuries for themselves, you can never say that I don't have her wellbeing at the front of my mind Lass.'

'Why don't you treat yourself to a pair? Then you can keep up with the pace of things in the buildings.'

'A bit less of the cheek would do very nicely young lady. I've worn clogs all my life and I can't remember losing my footing once. Besides, I like to take my time and be sure that the job is done right. But I'm interested in this delicate member of your mother's family. I want to know why she's decided that the very day that we're going to be busy thinning a few turnips is the best day she can choose to come here.'

'Is that you grumbling about our May again?' exclaimed Edith as she bustled back into the kitchen.

'I hear she's in a delicate state of health,' volunteered Jackson as he reached for another piece of dried bread to mop up his bacon fat.

Edith stopped abruptly in her tracks.

'What is wrong with her? Who told you she's ill?'

'Calm down Mother, it's only Dad deliberately misunderstanding me when I said that she only comes here in the good weather, we can't expect her to fight her way here through rain and snow.'

'Quite right! I would never forgive myself if she caught a feverish chill because she visited us.'

'Come and sit down for a few minutes Mother, here's a cup of tea.'

'Thanks! Esther … I think those pigs are getting too strong for me to feed, it's time they were sent to be butched, they're big enough, folks don't like their bacon to be too fat these days.'

Jackson snorted his disapproval as he carefully wiped the warm fat from his chin.

'I've never set foot in that doctor's surgery yet … and it's mostly due to all the fat bacon I've eaten every morning for years,' he looked Esther squarely in the eye as he continued.

'Have you ever known me have a sniffle of cold? Answer me that.'

Esther thought for a moment.

'No, I haven't, but you don't spend any time in stuffy rooms where you are more likely to pick up infections. I was reading an article in the paper last week where a famous doctor was saying that colds and 'flu' have nothing to do with being cold or wet, but the infection is spread by us breathing in germs which fly from one person to another.'

'It wasn't the Farmers Weekly you were reading was it? Surely you know better than to believe much of what you read in that!'

'Of course it wasn't. I rarely read any farming papers; it only makes me jealous when I see photos of smartly dressed farmers being interviewed in spotless yards with sparkling new machines in the background.'

Jackson shook his head sadly.

'I never thought a daughter of mine would be taken in by such false publicity, I thought I'd taught you that muck is healthy … any clean farmyard is a very suspicious place. Plenty of cow muck means that everything is working well. There's a natural order to things … anybody who can waste time scraping about and digging up cobbles then laying down concrete, must be neglecting what's going on with his stock and what's happening in his fields.'

'Don't you think it's about time you went to see that things are working well in your fields this morning, then you'll be back in time to have a few words with our May while you're having your dinner.'

'Can't I take a bit of bait with me then I needn't come home to bother you with my crack, in her delicate state it could be the end of her!'

'No! You can't take sandwiches… the turnip field is only across the road, she can easily see you from the kitchen window … she'd consider it an insult if you were to sit in that far dyke-back where she can watch you eat while we're sitting at the kitchen table!'

'She'll be insulted however hard I try to please her; that woman goes out of her way to take offence.'

Jackson hurried to join the impatient tail-wagging Patch.

'Thank goodness he's gone, I can get on with my work for a couple of hours.'

Esther nodded.

'At least I'll miss part of her visit, I'm going to the dentist this afternoon. I don't upset her as much as Dad does, but it's hard not to say something she disapproves of.'

'Well May, it's nice to see you,' said Jackson as he took his place wearily at the table, later that morning.

MUCK AGAIN!

'You seem unable to stand up straight today Jackson. I should think it's the result of wasting a few hours in the 'Grey Mare' last night, the good Lord has his own ways of punishing those who flaunt His laws too often.

Aunt May's swinging earrings glinted self-righteously.

'I've been crawling along them bone-dry stitches thinning turnips …' bubbled Jackson indignantly.

'Is that what you were doing?' interrupted a surprised May. 'I could see you kneeling on the ground fiddling with some little plants and I thought that you'd decided to have an easy day.'

'Easy day!' spluttered Jackson, 'you should try crawling on your hands and knees with bloody dust filling your eyes and being forced to swallow mouthfuls of the stuff if the slightest wind gets up!'

'There's no need to swear Jackson, I'm sure May understands how hard you work.'

'A lot of it seems unnecessary to me! I saw that nice Mister Steel working in his field when I walked here from the bus stop. He was riding on a smart shiny tractor which was pulling some sort of brightly painted machinery up and down his field. I could hear him singing as he worked, it was very pleasant to walk past a farmer who has time to be cheerful and courteous.'

'He doesn't know you well enough,' muttered Jackson sourly.

'What did you say Jackson?'

'You don't know him well enough, he's too bloody lazy to crawl up the stitches doing the job properly, he just grubs them at top speed sitting on that heap of expensive tin … waving to every passer-by he can spot on the road! Just you wait till I'm digging up my grand turnips while he's trying to sell his tiny scrappy things that have been nearly choked to death. It'll take half a dozen of his to make a decent pan of soup.'

'Be careful what you say about our neighbours Jackson. It's always best to keep on good terms with them, you never know when we may need their help.'

'Very wise Edith, a skilful farmer with a fine tractor is a local asset, you never know when one of your horses might die. That Peggy sniffs the air when I pass close to her as though she's about to cough, I've heard that horses can catch pneumonia easily … and death is quick. Anyway, she must be as old as me, I've often seen her leaning her back-end on the field gate … and she's always resting one or other of her hooves … I'm sure that's a bad sign.'

Jackson's temper had risen steeply as his sister-in-law in her usual judgemental tone delivered this unequivocal observation.

To Edith's relief, Esther breezed in.

Her aunt looked at her approvingly.

'You look very smart this morning Esther, are you going to Egremont?'

'Yes, I have an appointment with the dentist.'

Her aunt's face changed abruptly.

'Have you been to that dentist before?'

'Yes, but only for a check-up, there was nothing to be done then, but I've been getting some pain lately, so I thought I'd better have things checked over again. Do you go to a dentist in Whitehaven?' she asked politely.

Her aunt shook her head disdainfully.

'I wouldn't go to any dental practice where there was only one dentist, I prefer to have a choice.'

MUCK AGAIN!

'I should think they're all the same. Just so long as they don't hurt me I don't care how many are in the practice. I can easily bike to Egremont, but it's more difficult to travel as far as Whitehaven.'

'Oh, my poor girl! You don't know the first thing about how to choose a dentist!'

Jackson's interest had been rekindled by May's remarks. Feeling he should contribute something to a conversation which was rapidly moving out of his sphere of expertise, he felt moved to throw in a few words.

'I've never visited a dentist in my life! Edith went to see one a few times, but she carried on for days afterwards about how painful it had been when she'd had a few teeth pulled out, so I decided that I could deal with a simple matter like a bit of discomfort in the mouth by myself.'

'So what did you do Dad when you had toothache? It's a terrible thing to suffer.'

'All the pain will disappear after a while my girl. Once the tooth has broken to pieces the best thing is to scrape what's left out. I've always done it with a good pair of scissors. I can safely say that my gums let me eat anything, while folks with false teeth have to pick and choose what they put into their mouths.

Esther shivered at the thought of easing bits of tooth out with a pair of scissors. I can safely say that my gums let me eat anything, while folks with false teeth have to be fussy about what they eat.'My false teeth are beautiful Jackson,' May smiled proudly in his direction.

MUCK AGAIN!

MUCK AGAIN!

'Yes Dad, it must be awful to have no teeth in your mouth ... I couldn't live with only gums to smile with!'

Jackson chuckled

'Only folks who talk a lot and grin at strangers need to have fancy teeth in their mouths. If I had a set I wouldn't be able to remember where on earth I'd put the bloody things! There's plenty of chaps I know who've leaned over the side of a tractor and dropped their best teeth under the wheels. Now an old mare like Peggy would have spotted anything strange flying about and would have had the sense to stop faster than any tractor can change its gears.

'She stops every chance she gets when I work with her, she doesn't wait long enough to spot any flying teeth. A bit of a

cough or a tiny stone rattling against my clog is enough to halt her in mid-stride,' laughed Esther, 'but I must be off.'

'Just a minute, I wouldn't want a niece of mine to go unprepared into a dental surgery without having some sound advice to call upon.'

'Any advice would be acceptable Aunt May,' said her niece diplomatically.

'How can any of us give her advice about a subject none of us knows anything about?' snapped Jackson feeling that he was out of his depth again.

'Yes Jackson, there is much to bear in mind when a visit to these professional men is on the cards.

She turned to Esther.

'I noticed that you said that you don't mind who treats you just so long as the treatment doesn't hurt. Now that is the first mistake you can make.'

'How's that?' asked an astonished Esther, 'I certainly don't want to be hurt.'

Her aunt shook her head vehemently, her sparking earrings drunkenly endorsing her point of view.

'No my dear, I've had a great deal of painless treatment, but I'm sad to say that I've lost most of my upper teeth. However, my lower ones, which have had one or two painful fillings are as good as ever.'

She shook her finger in Esther's amazed direction.

'Mark my words ... any dentist who doesn't hurt you has no idea what he's doing!'

'But, wasn't it the same dentist who did all your treatment?'

'No, my first dentist died and then a young man joined the practice and gave me the painless treatment. And ... mark my words ... he was instrumental in the loss of my upper set.'

'That's right May, these youngsters won't put up with the slightest discomfort,' nodded Jackson in one of the rare moments when he felt he could agree with his bossy sister-in-law.

Edith smiled and nodded approval hoping that the conversation had survived another critical stage.

Jackson rose from the table as Esther's departing chuckle faded into the yard.

'Never mind May, you can come and grit your fancy teeth any day in my turnip field!'

'You are as ignorant of the finer things as ever Jackson Strong, I've no idea what made our Edith marry a man like you!' 'Maybe she fancied marrying a proper man instead of a stuffed shirt like the one you captured,' he murmured as the door closed behind him.

MUCK AGAIN!

'I didn't quite catch what he said Edith.'

'I'm sure it wasn't anything untoward; it's a shame but I don't think you have the knack of bringing out the best in him.'

Aunt May reached for her hat and carefully pushed a long ornate hatpin through both the hat and her beautifully permed hair. She gazed at her reflection for a moment in the small shaving mirror by the door then turned to her sister.

'Well Edith, whatever you saw in him is well hidden from the rest of us, all my friends have a certain amount of gentility … but of course I can't choose my relatives,' she said tartly as she swept out of the farmhouse.

'I can say exactly the same thing,' said Edith to herself as soon as she heard the farm dogs chorus her sister safely out of the farmyard.

2.

TOURISTS

Jackson leant happily on the field gate watching his skittish heifers enjoying the spring sunshine. Patch and Flash rested their eager noses on the lower rail while both tails swished expectantly as they eyed the huge animals they had just driven to this distant field.

Neither of them could begin to understand why some cows lumbered clumsily and had to be encouraged to move along at all, whilst these funny sort of cows had galloped along the main road leading the two dogs on a merry chase. The dizzy animals had managed to bring a fair number of cars and lorries to a halt as they'd frisked from the farm to this far meadow.

They gasped and panted, their long tongues dangling and dripping from tired mouths, all four eyes were bright with satisfaction as they watched the giddy heifers exploring their new pasture.

'You lot can stay here now for a few months, you'll be out of the way and let the milking cows eat the grass nearer home,' the farmer said to the unheeding youngsters.

Jackson chuckled to himself as he remembered the last time he had visited this field and had been surprised to find two botanists searching for wildlife in his useless wetlands.

He remembered the nights of entertainment he'd enjoyed in the Grey Mare on the strength of that totally unexpected meeting. A few pints had come his way as they had listened to his version of the encounter. Maybe

MUCK AGAIN!

Edith was right when she said that the good Lord always provides ... He had certainly provided a bit of fun. There was no chance that the same thing would happen again today.

The thought had scarcely left his mind when both dogs suddenly left their vantage point and raced off down the lonning, someone must be approaching.

Sure enough the slow figure of old Seth was making its way towards him. Flash and Patch rushed to greet the old man's two dogs ready to roll over and race alongside them. Their happy noise almost drowned the first words of the two old friends.

'I'm getting along only very slowly,' replied the older farmer in reply to Jackson's query.

'Aye old age comes to all of us ... if we're lucky!' nodded Jackson philosophically.

'Aye, aye, there's plenty who were killed down the pits and in the two world wars who would be only too pleased to suffer my bloody rheumatics!'

'What are you doing a good three miles from the village Seth?'

'I've come to have a look at our Harry's bullocks. I've got to help as much as I can, it takes a good hour or so out of his working day if he has to wander down here just to check on the young stock. I can still be useful even though I've turned eighty.'

'Just so long as you remember to tell folks where you're going before you set off. A chap could drop down dead here and wouldn't be likely to be found until mowing time.'

Seth chuckled.

MUCK AGAIN!

'You certainly know how to make a chap feel better about his old-age!'

'Well, us old folks have to come to an understanding about death, it's no use pretending that we'll live forever, especially the likes of us. We've both killed plenty of pigs, sheep and poultry ... so we can't expect death to hold back and wait for us to decide when we want to move on ... after all, we never asked a happy fat pig whether he was ready to be turned into bacon or not!'

Seth laughed heartily.

'Imagine living for another fifty years! You and me are ugly enough right now, I daren't think what a sight we'd be if we lived another thirty years or so!'

The two friends began to make their way slowly up the lonning towards the main road reminiscing as they went, but they hadn't gone very far before Seth decided to lean on a field gate to rest for a while. It happened to be one of John Steel's fields. Inside were a few young heifers grazing or lying down chewing the cud. It was a peaceful scene. But Jackson never missed a chance to criticise his modern-minded drinking companion.

'Just you look at them heifers Seth.'

'I can see them Jackson. Fine looking beasts; they should be a fair size in a few months on this good grazing and should be profitable milkers in a year or so.'

'No doubt they will be,' agreed Jackson, 'but it beats me how he can tell one heifer from another, these foreign breeds produce cattle that are identical to one another.'

'I think he has put tabs in their ears.'

'I think he bloody well needs to. Once these chaps decide to buy a foreign breed that has no special markings then it serves him right if has to go chasing his beasts round

18

the field to tell which one he's interested in. Thank God the bull has better ways of telling which cow is ready to be served. It's always man who complicates matters, not the animals.'

He expanded his thesis confidently.

'I can tell you Seth that I know my stock the minute they push their noses into this world. Once I see their markings I know who their grandmother is and a few generations before that. I don't need numbers in ears and stock books to know which of my beasts belong to which breeding line. Another thing, I can see at a glance if my young daft heifers have broken through the dyke to join somebody else's stock. John would have a struggle to recognize his colourless lot if they managed to muddle them selves up with a similar coloured herd.'

Jackson spat expertly past Flash's ears as if to underline his point. The dog stopped in her tracks in case her master had changed his mind about the general direction they were taking on this long warm afternoon. But no, he was probably checking that she knew he was there. She shook her head in exasperation then dashed ahead to see what Patch was sniffing at in the next gateway. Life on this sunny afternoon was very sweet for the two dogs. There were no great slow lumbering cows to direct homewards or skittish sheep to educate. Maybe at long last their master was beginning to realise that dogs like to roam free now and again, without constant shouts and fun-spoiling whistles.

Patch wagged his tail excitedly in total agreement. Being older than Flash he knew from long experience that when their master met another human being they were both free to romp and play for a while. Yes life could be good.

MUCK AGAIN!

'You know Jackson, I've no idea what I'd do if I hadn't this strong stick. Without it I'd have to sit around like an invalid just watching what's going on in the yard ... and our Harry says that I see too much as it is! So if I can only potter about he won't feel that I'm just sitting spying on him.'

'Aye, it's better to let him make his mistakes in private.' Seth paused again and settled himself in the dyke-back for another short rest. Jackson settled down companionably beside him.

After taking his roll of black twist from his pocket Jackson carefully pared a couple of slices from it and placed them gently on his tongue while Seth refilled his pipe and lit up.

'I can't understand why you ex-miners chew that stuff, a good warm draw on my pipe and I'm as right as rain.'

'Aye well, down the coal pits we couldn't light up like we did in the ore mines, so we learned how to chew black twist, it's just as good ... and saves lighting up in dangerous places like barns and byres. Besides, I don't have to remember to carry a box of matches in my pocket. When you were talking about your stick reminds me of when I went to spend a few days in the Lakes.'

Seth nodded expectantly as he knew that his old friend was an expert at telling a tale, even if it wasn't altogether true.

'I remember you telling us in the pub how, a good few years ago, you walked over the fells to spots like Langdale and Grasmere. Maybe you took a stick with you which has brought it all back to mind? You'd need one to help you clamber over them rough paths. It's a daft pastime if you ask me.'

MUCK AGAIN!

'You're right about that Seth. It's them southerners who come up here to wander about like a flock of herdwicks and risk their lives clambering about in spots where sensible folks never think of going. A wise shepherd always stands at the bottom of the fell and sends his dog over the high crags to look for the sheep.'

'But I thought that tourists brought money to them infertile valleys.'

Jackson nodded, then began to chuckle softly to himself.

'That reminds me of that very thing! They need money from the tourists over there as it's the wives who can let a room or two who make that bit of extra cash for the house.'

He eased himself into a more comfortable position as he settled to tell his tale. Seth waited expectantly.

'One day when I was wandering around the countryside, I found myself in Grasmere, you've heard of the place?'

'Aye, it's where they buried that poet, Wordsworth. I remember reading some thing about daffodils at school, but I was too busy thinking about the ratting I was going to do that night with my new ferret to pay attention to a bit of poetry. A damned good ferret it was an'all, just a pity it vanished down a long drainage pipe and I never saw it again.'

'That often happens, I reckon the little buggers taste freedom down there. They know you can't reach them so easy. No Seth, there's nowt as crafty as a little animal, the smaller they are the craftier they seem to be.'

Seth nodded agreement.

'Aye, but you were telling me about when you were in Grasmere years ago.'

MUCK AGAIN!

'That's right. It was the time when I was young and daft enough to go over the fells with Jimmy Marshall who'd got fed up with working up at Wasdale Head and decided to go back home to Grasmere.'

'I remember that lad very well. A lish sort of chap like most lads bred on the fells. He must have been homesick.' He rose stiffly to his feet.

'I'll have to walk on a bit or else I'll be stuck in this dyke-back for good."

'Come on then Seth, I'm not so keen to sit in this damp spot either.'

The two friends walked on companionably each leaning on his stick The startled dogs woke from their snoozes eager to race ahead again.

'Like I was saying,' continued Jackson, 'Jimmy was so pleased I'd walked over the passes with him that he was keen for me to stop a while over there and have a look round the famous Lake District villages. But it wasn't as quiet as Wasdale, the whole area was overrun with tourists. Most of them were foreign and seemed to us to have money to burn.' Seth nodded. 'As you can imagine, Jimmy knew every soul in Grasmere and the surrounding district and I'm pleased to say that he was welcome in all the pubs in the district.

So one day he took me into a hotel bang in the middle of Grasmere, we had a pint or two at the bar then made our way outside. The centre of the village was busy with tourists milling about and gazing at everything in the shops. As we walked past the front of a big hotel I noticed a chap sitting on the veranda in a rickety old rocking chair and smoking his pipe contentedly.

MUCK AGAIN!

'Who's that?' I asked Jimmy when we'd walked a little way down the road, 'he doesn't look like the sort to book into a posh hotel. Is he some sort of weird millionaire?' but Jimmy roared with laughter.

Seth paused for a minute then resumed his measured progress while Jackson continued his crack.

'He explained to me that he wasn't an eccentric millionaire, his name was Donald and had worked in the slate quarries when he'd been younger, but had found it hard graft. Then, after being injured in a roof fall he'd happened on an easy way of making a shilling or two.'

Jackson spat sharply with immense satisfaction into the powdery dust on the lonning floor then continued his reminiscences.

'Jimmy told me how one day Donald had been sitting at that very spot in the old rickety chair on the veranda holding his pint in one hand with the other resting lightly on his stick as he idly watched the visitors strolling by. Then all of a sudden, an American stopped to admire his walking stick which was only a knotted, rough-looking thing he'd cut from the dyke. This one here's a lot smarter.'

Jackson raised his stick into the air then continued.

'The wily chap sensed that there was money to be made if he played his cards right. Sure enough the visitor asked if it was for sale. His quick wit came to his aid as he explained that as he'd cut this stick from the yew tree which leans over Wordsworth's grave it was a very special one so he was loth to part with it.'

Seth bubbled with laughter as he realised what Donald had in mind.

MUCK AGAIN!

MUCK AGAIN!

'I've heard that them dalesmen can be pretty crafty when it comes to money, I bet he ended up selling the stick?'

'You're dead right there. Not only did he sell it for a price well beyond anything it was worth, but he quickly realised that selling Wordsworth sticks could keep him in bread and beer for the rest of his life.'

'It goes to show how daft tourists can be,' said Seth, 'wait until I tell our Maggie that tale, she thinks all Americans are like them film stars she sees in the picture house! Her favourite is a chap called John Wayne. She's convinced he's a proper cowboy, not a chap who's learned the words off by heart.'

'Aye well, women are easily taken in, but you haven't to let them know too much otherwise they'll start questioning our good judgement. A clever woman can be dangerous about a well-run farm. She's apt to pick up a copy of the 'Farmers Weekly' in an idle moment and latch onto some expensive improvement that she thinks we're short of. A slow reader or a woman with poor eyesight is a definite advantage to a struggling farmer. But like us all I wasn't that wise when I married our Edith. As it is, I have to make sure that all dangerous literature finds its way into the closet as soon as possible. That's the only reason I settle to read the farming magazines as soon as they come.'

'You're right Jackson, but I've trained Maggie very well, I think she's past the giddy stage now.'

By this time the friends had reached the main road where Jackson's two dogs dashed homewards barely glancing back certain that their master knew his way home without their help. Seth's dogs were already trotting homewards in the opposite direction sure that they would arrive there and have eaten their dinner long before their master reached home.

'Take care as you walk Seth, car drivers never seem to spot anything that moves slowly.

That's true enough, thought Jackson as he quickened his step to follow his non-existent dogs. But there's one thing for sure ... there'll always be the 'clever Dicks' who will take unsuspecting tourists for a ride ... but then ... it serves them right!

MUCK AGAIN!

3.

PET LOVERS

Edith stood uncertainly scanning the letter which had only just been delivered that morning. Jackson, unnerved by the silence, looked enquiringly at his pre-occupied wife.

'Something wrong?' he asked casually.

'Well, this is a strange letter, it's from a League of animal lovers of some sort.'

'Read it then, we're all animal lovers in this house. I couldn't earn a decent living unless I gave the best of care to all my animals. What do they want to know Edith? I expect it's more of them experts who are looking for the best farmers in the district to advise them on policy matters.'

'No, I think it's some form of R.S.P.C.A.'

'Who's that?'

'The Royal Society for the Prevention of Cruelty to Animals'

'Quite right, there should be a Society, especially a royal one. What do they want?'

They say they are launching a campaign to make the general public more aware of how animals are treated in the countryside. It goes on to say that there have been many complaints from walkers passing near farm land saying that some farm animals are thin, hungry or crippled. Some have even spotted cows and sheep limping painfully about in the fields.'

'Do they mean my stock Edith, if they have written to us? Have they also written to them farmers who crowd too

MUCK AGAIN!

many milking cows into small fields where the grass never manages to grow to a decent length because it's overgrazed?'

'No, this letter hasn't been sent to you alone. It says that it's a circular letter informing all farmers that the general public will be encouraged to report any stock that they may consider to be cruelly treated or neglected ... to them immediately.'

Edith folded the letter carefully and placed it behind the tea caddy on the mantelpiece.

'What are you putting the letter up there for? Do you intend to answer it?'

'No, but I thought I'd better keep it handy.'

'Well you can just take it down from there and throw the bloody thing in the fire.'

'But it's an official letter,' stammered Edith, flustered by her husband's disregard of a missive from such a well-known Society.

Jackson's temper was beginning to rise as he reflected on the threat expressed in the letter.

'Throw it on the fire,' he repeated 'they have a bloody cheek writing to folks like me who've treated the stock better than we've treated ourselves.'

He swept his arm expansively over the table as he warmed to his topic.

'Who have you treated better than you've treated the family?' asked Bill as he entered the kitchen ready for his breakfast, 'not that I've time to wait until we add them all up.'

'What do you mean by a daft remark like that?' asked his irate father.

MUCK AGAIN!

'As far as I can see, the family comes last if there's money or days off to be handed around, I can state categorically that the stock do very well on this farm.'

'There you are Mother, you can throw that letter where it belongs, the R.S.P.C. or whoever they are, they had to send me a letter just to make it look fair. Your own son has just admitted that our stock is ruined and treated like pets. Wasn't the word cruelty somewhere among them sentences?'

'Yes, it was … but it's only hoping to prevent cruelty, not telling farmers that they are cruel to their beasts.'

'I should think not!'

'But Dad, you misunderstood me. The fact that we are less important than the animals, doesn't mean to say that the stock is treated well by you. It's just that you make money out of them so they need more consideration than we do.'

'What on earth are you saying? Don't talk in riddles, you make less sense than that letter your mother is too frightened to burn.'

Edith opened the letter again and turned to her son.

'This letter is from the R.S.P.C.A. and warns us farmers that the public is to encouraged to spot any cases of cruelty they might see in the countryside and report them to the Society.'

Bill nodded.

'Let's hope they can spot suffering farmers' sons and daughters as well.'

Jackson snorted.

'I don't have the money to pay you a top wage, besides your time's your own when it's raining, there's not many jobs where you can spend most of the winter sitting in front of the fire talking about the neighbours and all their goings-on.'

Bill laughed at the thought.

'How about milking twice every day ... and all the machinery we have to paint when the weather's bad? And the walls to be repaired ... and the whitewashing, to say nothing of the broken fences that need to be fixed?'

'Just you leave the whitewashing alone. The last time you whitewashed the byre walls you cleaned off all the serving dates I'd written up there. Suddenly good milkers were drying off, and newborn calves were appearing alongside unexpected mothers in the mornings, seemingly from nowhere! It took your mother a couple of years to sort just what stock we had. She even threatened to pack in the bookkeeping ... and that would have been the end of any letter writing to the Ministry from this house.'

'I'm glad that at last you realise how much I do for this farm,' snapped Edith 'if I didn't do it for you, it would serve you right if you were taken to court for not returning official forms to them! Just you bear it in mind that all the paper work has to be completed even it's pouring down ... or whether it's winter or summer!'

'I'd better keep quiet or I'm likely to be sent to jail ... and who will look after the farm then?'

'Don't talk so daft Jackson, you'd have to learn about book-keeping just like I had to do.'

Jackson ignored her pointed remark and continued more reflectively.

'But I think we'd better watch what we're doing if a lot of spying, nosey-parkers are going to be let loose in the country-side to make sure that we coddle our stock in the same way that townsfolk pamper their pets!'

MUCK AGAIN!

He was now warming to his new topic.

'They tell me that in the towns and cities there are vets who only treat cats and dogs!'

He turned to Edith in disdain.

'We couldn't even round up the half-wild cats we have in the barns let alone check to see if our rat population is fit and healthy!

Bill laughed at the thought.

'Aye they'd have to be able to run faster than a frightened rat if they plan to examine any of the barn cats! But most of our pet cats can only catch a rat if they creep up on it first. Mind you our rats are so well fed that if they get a whisker ahead of any of the cats they are safe enough!'

'Yes Bill, you've been going on about keeping the meal and feed in metal bins, but I'm not made of money lad. But just you remember that if the rats can't get a feed fairly easily they'll be arriving into the house, there are far too many scraps left lying about in here. Yes, we've the healthiest rats in the district, sleek and fat they are … the same as all our stock.'

'That's nothing to boast about Jackson. I've begged you to fill in the holes in the walls for years, but it's always promises and more promises. No doubt you'll wait until one of your sleek rats decides it wants to join us in here for better things!'

'It needn't bother itself,' laughed Bill to himself, 'I reckon it has more choice out in the buildings!'

Luckily his mother was busy trying to make the offending letter catch fire.

MUCK AGAIN!

MUCK AGAIN!

'But seriously Dad, we'll have to check the stock in the far fields a bit more regularly, just to make sure everything's all right. A day can make such a difference, especially if a heifer gets stuck on barbed wire or manages to break through a dyke.'

His father looked up sharply.

'The day you remember to check any stock that's out of sight of the farmyard will be the day that history'll be made in this farm. It's only me and the two dogs who give a damn about what might happen a mile or more from the house.'

'Come on Dad!' chuckled Bill mischievously, 'you seem to have forgotten a couple of years back when you had a few young heifers and couple of what you thought were old dry cows out of the way in the far meadows near Thornhill. When eventually you found the time to go and check them … there was old Daisy, not with just one calf … but twins!'

'Anyone can make a mistake,' soothed Edith as Jackson threatened to burst a blood vessel.

'A mistake?' roared Bill, 'the only one to make a mistake was the old bull we had then. I knew he was finding the young heifers too much for him, he could only catch old Daisy on a good day. Thank God we've booked into the new AI service.'

'You young clever chaps might laugh, but I'm still waiting for that vet to produce a set of twins. Good money thrown after bad if you ask me. Besides, if some folks wipe my serving dates off the barn wall it throws all my breeding plans out.'

'And another thing' continued Bill mercilessly, 'what if one of your retired ewes drops dead in a corner of one of them far fields? The smell would soon attract one of them botanical chaps looking for wetlands and wild flowers. Those sort of experts can smell anything unusual much quicker than uneducated folks like us. Wetlands!' he chuckled gleefully. 'That's what them two experts called that stinking swamp; but a couple of dead sheep wouldn't half add a flavour to things, but I doubt they would enthuse about rotting mutton among the water lilies!'

Edith shifted about her kitchen uneasily.

'I think it's time you both found some work to do outside, the calves are bawling their heads off.'

'Aye well, maybe we'd better feed them up a bit more if it keeps your mother's face straight. I'm off to put a notice up in the field next to the railway station before the summer passengers start arriving.'

'What notice?' asked Edith alarmed.

'The 'BEWARE OF THE BULL' notice we took down when we got rid of the old bull.'

'What's the use of putting the notice back up when we have no bull?' laughed Bill as he picked up his cap.

'I don't want any busy-bodies poking their noses around the stock, they won't know which are bulls and which are bullocks, so when they read the notice they'll decide to walk on the main road instead of taking the short cut through the field. The Society for cruelty will have to get up early in the morning if they want to inspect my stock looking for crippled or dying animals.'

*　　　　*　　　　*

'There's no need to send a letter like that to our farm,' announced John Steel as Jean, the barmaid, placed a second pint in front of him. 'The likes of us who show our new breeds in all the big agricultural shows set a fine example to the farming community of what a healthy well-bred animal looks like.'

'I'm sure that letter is intended to make the general public more aware of what fine beasts can be spotted in this area. The ordinary man in the street doesn't really know what a healthy dairy cow looks like, it has to be lying flat on its back before they notice that anything's wrong,' agreed Harry Jepson knowingly.

'If that's the case then you'll have to keep a closer eye on your cows Jackson,' observed John glancing casually in the direction of the old farmer who was enjoying his game of cards near the fire, seemingly oblivious of the subject under discussion.

'Most of your old cows suffer from some sort of arthritis, even the vet won't have treated farm stock with diseases of old age, I manage to butch ours before they begin to feel their years!'

Jackson slowly and deliberately finished his hand before deciding to address the waiting drinkers.

'Have you chaps any idea of the money I've made from my ageing stock? Whilst the likes of John have bought, sold and trained a procession of new milking cows to find their way around your byres, mine have quietly gone about their business for a good many fruitful years.'

He paused to gather the reaction to his words, then continued his argument.

'My cows know their stalls like ...'

'Like you know your way home from the pub after dark interrupted John slyly.

'You might say that. It's a good thing to have your animals able to sort themselves out on a cold winter's morning without any guidance when you've had a bit of a late night in here.'

'Quite right,' murmured Tom Graham as he handed the waiting pints around.

'Well-trained stock is less work all round,' continued Jackson thoughtfully, 'they can read my mind like a book. They know exactly how much they can get away with. That Maud knows when to settle herself down just by listening to my clogs on the cobbles outside the byre door.'

'I've heard your Bill say the same thing about your moods in the mornings. He knows whether to speak or to keep his head down when he hears your clogs crossing the yard first thing in the morning!'

'A pack of bloody lies! He's too late getting out of bed to beat me to the byre door of a morning. And … I would have thought busy neighbours would have little time to quiz my family about my early morning habits, it's a right job when a chap can hardly go to his water closet in peace without the whole district knowing about it.'

John grinned at the thought.

'We're only warning you about the state of some of your stock. To the townie they'll look starved, they won't know anything about geriatric milking cows. You'll have to plough up all of your fields which border the roadside in case a wandering tourist is checking his hit list. Doubtless you will have heard that they're providing guidelines for the townsfolk to follow, they'll all be experts.'

'We'll see who'll be the ones to be reported, jealousy is a very destructive thing,' retorted Jackson as the chorus of laughter swept through the Grey Mare.

MUCK AGAIN!

Edith looked up from her copy of the Whitehaven News and smiled in her husband's direction.

'You look like a cat's that pinched the cream, surely there can't be anything in the paper to be so pleased about?

'Just you listen to this ... fell walkers were praised last week by the R.S.P.C.A for drawing attention to the high quality of animal husbandry witnessed in the Lake District. The Society congratulates itself on the initiative it has shown in educating town-based tourists the ways of the countryside'.

Jackson chuckled to himself.

'None of them can have wandered about around here then!'

'What do you mean Jackson?'

'Well, last week I went down Anchor Lonning. I thought that it was decided that Bill was going to check the stock down there, but when I asked him how things were, he said that he thought that I'd agreed to look after things.'

'Good heavens! If I don't check after the pair of you anything is likely to happen.'

'So, when at last I managed to get down there what did I see?'

Edith shivered at the thought.

'Some visitor to the famous wetlands had left the gate partly open and two of the thinnest heifers were larking about with that young pedigree bull in Alan Steel's field. God knows how many pounds he paid for it, I heard that it's a French breed and the cost of transporting the bull from over there has sent him into debt for the next five years.'

MUCK AGAIN!

'It'll be a good investment if the calves sell well, they say that those French breeds are going to be the best money-making stock soon in this country.'

'Where have you been reading all this Edith?'

'Somebody's got to read the Farmers Weekly.'

'Well we'll soon know.'

'What do you mean by we'll soon know?'

'Them two heifers weren't swapping thoughts about the state of the weather with that sprightly bull!'

'Oh Jackson! You must pay Alan for the services.'

'The heifers are back where they belong and who's to notice any difference when the calves are born? Mine have always come in a good array of colours.'

'The man isn't daft! Wait until he spots them in our fields, he'll want compensation.'

Jackson laughed.

'Two roan heifers can throw any mix of colours Edith! You know ... it was a good thing that the cruelty Society got us into a bit of a muddle, it's helped us to become one of the first farms in the north of England to go international!'

4.

RAMBLING

'Y ou're going where?'
'Rambling Dad, I've joined a rambling club.'
'Good God! Doesn't rambling mean walking about aimlessly?'

'No, all my friends feel that we know very little about the busier parts of the Lake District. If anybody were to ask us about Ullswater or Tarn Hows, most of us wouldn't have a notion what they look like let alone explaining how to get there.'

Jackson shook his head in disbelief.

'Who would be likely to ask you a daft question like that when you live half a day's journey from them parts?'

'You never know Dad, just think of all these new people who are coming to work at Sellafield, they will want to explore the area and look to us to provide information about what's on offer in our own county.'

She reached for a shopping bag as she spoke and pulled out a shoebox.

'These are a pair of proper walking boots I've bought to wear on the rough paths. Everybody is advised to buy a stout pair as well as buying waterproof trousers and jacket.'

Jackson stared as his daughter unwrapped her new clothes for his inspection.

'Who paid for all them new clothes?'

'I helped her,' announced Edith, 'she should have a good hobby where she can meet new friends and enjoy a day out.

MUCK AGAIN!

'And what about her bus fare to these far-flung places.'

'I can just afford it on the money you pay me ... but only just! I think I'm due a little rise. After all, I've worked hard in the fields for the last few weeks, I deserve a bit extra.'

'I'm not subsidising reckless expense on clothing that you don't need! It was only a week or so ago that I gave you money to buy a new pair of strong clogs to work in the fields ... and what did you do? You went off and bought yourself a pair of them newfangled wellington boots!' He paused for breath. 'Of course I blame you Edith for encouraging her! You set a bad example when you bought a pair last year.'

'Everybody wears wellies now Dad, I can't be seen working on the farm wearing old-fashioned clogs that clatter. I made more noise than the horses. Besides, it's all too easy to slip with ancient caulkers on the soles.'

'Aye, but let something drop onto the rubber toes and it'll feel like you're wearing carpet slippers.' After a moment's reflection he expanded his argument.

'Could you earn any money at all with a broken foot strapped up in a heavy plaster? You'd be sitting on the sofa all day expecting your mother to wait on you hand and foot. God knows how we'd manage to set the taties and do the milking every day with the two of you out of commission!'

'You always think of the worst thing that could happen if any one of us thinks of doing anything different,' grumbled Esther, 'it was the same when we spent a few days in Coniston last year. You carried on about how you'd been neglected, trying to make us both feel a bit guilty ... until I had a word with Mary Graham ... and she said that you'd spent every evening over at their house enjoying the best suppers you said you'd had for years!'

'A chap has to look after himself as best he can when he's neglected by his own family who decide to go gallivanting off to spots only folks who have nowt better to do at home and are daft enough, visit on a regular basis.'

'It's nice to see the family once in a while Jackson, it's a welcome change from the thankless work we do here,' snapped Edith 'you go off this Sunday Esther, we'll manage quite well for one day. You might even meet a nice young man.'

Jackson glanced up sharply from the paper he'd only just picked up.

'What's wrong with the Young Farmers' Club? I hear that one or two young farming folks have tied the knot after they met there.'

'Maybe I can do better than marry a farmer's son, I want to get away from the muck and low-paid work on a farm like this.'

'You don't know when you're well off young lady. I expect you have your eyes set on capturing one of them clever atom workers at Sellafield! Well, just take care … we know all about a local lad, but them fancy chaps who travel across the country from one job to another can have any sort of dodgy background. Believe me a decent farmer's son is worth a dozen of their kind.'

'I think I can spot a wrong'un by now Dad. Don't worry about me I'll bring you a slab of Kendal Mint Cake to sweeten you up.'

MUCK AGAIN!

MUCK AGAIN!

Jackson spotted Alan Steel's tractor coming towards him along the narrow road 'damn him and his bloody big tractor' he said to himself as he pulled Peggy to an unwilling halt as his neighbour drew to a stop alongside him.

'Soon there won't be room on these narrow roads for both horses and tractors,' said Alan breezily.

'Aye, this daft horse has trailed about the field all morning as if she has no energy left, but once I point her nose towards home she behaves as if she's entered for the four-thirty at Carlisle.'

'I'll tell you what Jackson, as you have no motor car, if you fancy going to the races you'll have to ride her there. One day you'll waken up to the fact that cars and tractors are the up-to-date machinery. Notice how my tractor is no trouble, it stands still while your Peggy is more than ready to have a go at climbing up the dyke to get home … she's nearly pulling your arms out of their sockets!'

Jackson pulled tighter on the reins as his mare threatened to push past the growling tractor.

'I'll make up my own mind about how I'll waste my own money,' snapped Jackson.

'I've just seen your Esther leaving your yard dressed up in walking gear. I would have thought that she'd have done enough tramping about on the farm that she'd never fancy a walking weekend! But I suppose there's no way of knowing what flights of fancy young lasses take these days.'

Aware that his wily neighbour was being provocative Jackson reached into his pocket to take out his penknife and a roll of black twist. He deliberately cut a slice and placed it on his tongue before replying, knowing fine well that anything he said was likely to be repeated with blandishments in the Grey Mare.

'The fact is, our Esther hasn't been so busy these last few weeks, I must have been easy on her ... and she must have a lot of spare energy. Besides, it'll do the lass good to see what the rest of the county's like. I believe she's off over to Grasmere with a rambling club of some sort, so she should settle to a bit of harrowing next week.'

Alan nodded reflectively.

'Provided her feet aren't blistered! And have you thought that she might meet a chap from Whitehaven or maybe another town, such folks like to get out into the countryside at the weekend, town bred lads can seem very smart to a lass brought up on a rough farm.'

'Aye well, we'll have to wait and see Alan, young folks marry who they fancy just like we did. But my tea'll be ready and this mare's belly thinks her throat's cut.'

'As he drove on Alan chuckled to himself, in spite of Jackson's casual manner he felt he'd given the old farmer something to think about.

*   *   *

Later that evening Jackson entered the kitchen enjoying the smell of his fried supper which had drifted over the yard and into the byre making him hurry the last minute feeding.

'What on earth is wrong with you?' he asked his daughter who was seated by the fire with both feet soaking in a bowl of steaming water.

'My feet are killing me.'

MUCK AGAIN!

'I told you that you could do as much walking as you like here at home without crippling yourself in some wild spot a half day's bus journey away. I can't understand young folks today who want to punish themselves for nothing. Now if you'd had sore feet after doing a long day's harrowing I would have sympathised.'

'It wasn't for nothing Dad, the view from the top of Helvellyn was pure magic, but the mountain we went up before that had such a cute name, it's called Dollywagon. I wonder why it's called that.'

'God knows! There's not much sense about them Lake District names; often it's to outwit the tourists. There's nothing like putting a daft question into their minds to keep them guessing ... and to keep the locals thinking up an equally daft answer.'

'You should have seen that dangerous ridge called Striding Edge, it made shivers run down my spine!'

'I reckon a pair of bad feet's enough without ruining your back as well. How do you think you're going to follow a pair of horses and a set of harrows tomorrow if you're crippled from head to toe? I think it would be better if you worked in a field a long way from the main road, I don't want all the neighbours sniggering about the state you're in, they might report me to them cruelty folk.'

'You talk a lot of nonsense Jackson!' snapped Edith, 'if she can't walk tomorrow she'll stay at home.'

Jackson shook his head as he settled at the table for his supper.

'I should have broken my boots in at home for a week or two, then they would have been OK so now I'll wear them in the fields until they're comfortable.'

MUCK AGAIN!

Jackson looked at her in dismay.

'You mean you're going to dress up to work in the fields! That'll give the neighbours something to laugh about. I make

a big thing about the poverty we have to endure ... and then you walk into the fields looking like an alpine mountaineer. Once I saw pictures of them in a Geographical Magazine, they were kitted out to withstand sub-zero temperatures and long nights sitting on a glazier. In fact they were wearing less than you had on this morning! All you need is a course in yodelling and we're all set for tying bells round the cows' necks. Do you want to make us the laughing stock of the district?'

'You're talking rubbish again Jackson. Esther can't dress like a rough farmhand when she mixes with nice folks like those in the Whitehaven Rambling Club.'

Esther signalled her mother to stop.

'At least she doesn't come home crippled from farm work. And as for you Edith, you're beginning to sound like your May when you go on about nice folks in the rambling club, downright snobbery if you ask me.'

'My feet were often sore from the lumps of hard soil and tiny pebbles that got into my clogs before I managed to persuade you to let me wear wellies.'

' If they're all that good why didn't you wear them to go up Helvellyn?'

Esther didn't bother to reply as she gingerly dried her feet, taking care to hide her large blisters from her father's beady eyes. Suddenly she remembered something.

'Apart from thoroughly enjoying the day Dad, I had a new experience.'

'What was that then? Did you injure another part of you?'

'No, but I got the surprise of my life when I opened the first gate we came to.'

'Why was that then?'

'I automatically heaved my shoulder under the rail to lift it up to open it ... but it swung open at a touch! So did all the others we went through! Every gate had two hinges and a proper sneck. It's been a great day today.'

Jackson shook his paper open and turned towards the fire muttering to himself.

'It's a bloody good day when a daughter of mine has, at long last, managed to learn how to open a gate!'

5.

IN THREES

Jackson cursed to himself as he leant over the pen and watched the sow feeding her new-born piglets. He hesitated to describe it as a litter, because this young gilt had produced only three little pigs at her first farrowing. She grunted proudly as she shifted her body to accommodate her snuggling babies.

'You mustn't put yourself out,' he remarked aloud to the sow, 'you've so many spare tits that these little buggers'll have their work cut out emptying all of them.'

Three had been born yesterday evening and he'd hoped that the pig would produce a few more during the night, but even though he'd searched under every bit of straw and poked in the far corners of the hull, the young mother had only presented him with these three.

He couldn't understand it. After all, her mother and grandmother were still giving birth to large litters. In addition he'd bought a new boar to stop any in-breeding, it was all expense. But he couldn't blame the boar, this wasn't his first litter. No, somewhere along the line there was a fault ... but it was a fault he'd soon irradicate. He turned back to the sow.

'I'll give you one more chance young lady, and if you give me an afterthought like this again it'll be the slaughterhouse for you. I daren't even sell you through the open market in case the buyer comes back to complain if you're set on breeding triplets. I'd never live it down.'

MUCK AGAIN!

He walked away muttering to himself ... 'three bloody pigs! Thank goodness the war's over, I wouldn't have dared put only one piglet born, in the stock book! The Ministry would never have believed that any animal with a milk bar as long as this one could produce only one tiny offspring!'

Norah grunted happily as her owner closed the pig hull door ... for her, life was a long line of comfortable pleasures.

Ten minutes later as Jackson shouted the cows to come into the byre to be milked he heard the door slam smartly against the wall.

'That's the third time that daft Rosebud has slammed her way into the byre,' he said to Bill who was busy tying up the cows.

'That's because Patch is too sharp on them and pushes them through the door too fast, you forget that she's in-calf and is likely to get jammed if she's rushed.'

'I'm not likely to forget she's in-calf, but I can't see her calving date because somebody made himself busy and whitewashed my serving dates off the byre wall.'

'Have you never heard of hygiene Dad? We're supposed to keep everything spotless if we deal with dairy products.'

'Aye, I've heard of hygiene. But the milk is safe enough inside the cows, then it goes straight into the bucket and from there into the cooler. I don't allow anybody to wash the walls down with it on this farm! I don't know what on earth you're talking about, our milk is as good as anybody else's. In fact these cows are so well fed and well treated that the quality of milk is the best you can buy.

49

Only folks with skinny cows which give thin milk have anything to worry about.'

'There's no explaining things to Dad, you're stuck in the nineteenth century.'

'I've managed to live a long way through this one, so I can't be so unhygienic ... and, who gave her a name like Rosebud? She's more like an overgrown cabbage.'

Rosebud pressed herself against the wall as Jackson squeezed his bulk between her and the pole in the middle of the stall.

'If she gets any fatter I'll have to cut this bloody pole out of the stall,' he said as he emerged gasping for breath. I must have miscalculated somewhere, she should have calved by now, if she waits much longer she'll have to stop outside, we don't have a doorway she can get through.'

'How many more pigs did Norah have this morning then?' asked Bill wishing to change the subject.

'Norah, you call her? No bloody good would be a better name. She still has only three, the same as last night. They'll have to thrive at some pace if we're to make a profit out of them, just think of the expense of the feed! We'll have to charge caviar prices for their bacon if we're to get any money back at all.'

Bill felt sorry for the sow which they'd reared from birth.

'She's only a young sow, maybe she'll do better next time.'

'Aye, maybe, but I'll put her in a pen with her mother for a bit, she'll maybe get the idea.'

Bill laughed heartily as he began putting the milking clusters onto the cows.

'Wouldn't it be better putting her with that new boar again, maybe a bit more time together will do the trick?'

MUCK AGAIN!

'Yes I'll do that, but I'll still put her in a pen with an older sow for a bit.'

'Why's that?' asked a puzzled Bill.

'Well you know how boars sing to the sow beforehand?'

'Aye.'

'Well, God knows what they whisper, but I reckon her mother understood and can give her a lot more useful advice than that daft young boar. Somewhere along the line there's been a misunderstanding.'

'I've never heard of such stupid talk!' exclaimed an astonished Bill.

'Don't you tell me what's daft and what isn't. Let's both wait and see if our ideas work better the next time … and, another thing Bill, don't you go telling our neighbours that the cat had a bigger litter of useless kittens than that well-bred sow managed to produce this morning.'

'I'll say nowt, unless somebody asks me, then I can't tell any lies.'

'You'll have to learn to do that lad. You only let folks know what's good for them, telling the truth often makes a chap into a laughing stock.'

He turned back to Rosebud who had laid herself down in the straw in her stall pleased that nobody would disturb her at milking time. 'Life's a line of comfortable pleasures' she thought to herself as she slowly began to chew her cud and move her ears languidly to monitor all the activity going on around her.

'If she eats any more she'll not be able to get up onto her feet. She's another example of how we spoil all our animals. She's not likely to bother to calve in a hurry if she can lie in her comfortable stall being fed on the best we can offer. Maybe we should leave her out in the field and let her wander about a bit more, that'll maybe encourage her muscles to get into gear.'

'Leave her alone Dad, you know fine well she'll pine if she's left by herself while the others are in here. That would amount to cruelty.'

'Don't be so daft lad, a bit of stress will liven her up a bit.'

Bill shook his head in despair. He shouldn't argue with his father, the old man had his own ideas ... and often he was right, but time would tell, both with the sow and the overdue cow.

*   *   *

Edith scattered the henfeed and smiled as the hungry hens flapped and squawked as they fought each other for a place closer to her bucket.

From the corner of her eye Edith was aware of the limping form of Hoppelty, a missing hen, who was joining the hungry throng. Hoppelty had once been brooding on a nest in the middle of a hayfield when the mowing machine had accidentally severed half of one leg. But the hen had never let such an incident stop her from laying her eggs in well-hidden places. Whenever she disappeared Edith knew that she would be busy brooding her own eggs.

Hoppelty had been such a good clocker that Edith had once placed duck eggs under her, but to the hen's alarm her new babies decided to take a swim whenever they came across a puddle. This inexplicable turn of events persuaded her to be very secretive about where she chose to lay her eggs.

Every spring the little hen and the farmer's wife were locked in a battle of wills. Edith searched all the unlikely places around the farm and in the nearby paddock. But the wily hen usually won! Who can say that hens are stupid?

Today Edith had a fair idea from which direction the hen had come. Leaving the flock to squabble and scratch among thems elves she hurried into the paddock and poked hopefully behind every gorse bush she came to. At last! She spotted the nest in a hole left by a dislodged cobble. Gingerly she reached into Hoppelty's hidey-hole. The tips of her fingers touched the warm eggs. She counted them. Hoppelty usually marched triumphantly into the farmyard with at least ten fluffy, squeaking chicks in tow. But no, she counted again ... only three! She couldn't believe what her fingers told her. She checked again. Sure enough, three warm cosy eggs lay in the centre of the feather-lined nest!

Edith returned to the farmyard amazed at this year's clutch. She wondered if a stoat had managed to steal some. Perhaps Hoppelty couldn't count?

Goodness, what was she thinking?

Animals can't count! She had credited the crafty Hoppelty with a great deal of intelligence; surely the hen knew that she wasn't sitting on as many eggs as usual?

The old hen scuttered under the field gate as Edith returned to the farmyard. As the two passed each other Edith was certain the hen's beady eye fixed her with a look as if to say I hope you haven't disturbed my eggs even though you've been clever enough to find them.

MUCK AGAIN!

Edith turned and watched as hoppelty disappeared into her hidden nest.

'I wonder if she's busy counting them to see whether I've pinched one!' she thought out aloud.

'Who are you talking to?' asked Jackson as he wheeled a load of muck out of the byre.

Jackson laughed when he heard the tale.

'Everything is happening in threes, I don't know whether it's good or bad luck!

'It'll be three o'clock before we get anything done today, I'll have to get a move on or the dinner will be late.'

'Three bloody pigs! Only three eggs! What else can come in a three? They say that troubles always come in threes, so I wonder what the third disaster will be! The only stock breeding well on this farm are the wild rabbits, I'd better set a few more snares tonight, that'll stop the little buggers prancing about and washing their ears only yards from where a chap is working.'

Back in the byre he stopped and thought aloud 'but tonight'll be a bright moonlit one when the crafty little things will be able to spot a snare from half way across the field!'

He shook his head reflectively. He was getting morbid in his old age. He must be when he was starting to think that the animals were becoming masters of their own destiny! He sighed and then attacked the cow muck with a renewed vigour.

*   *   *

Early the next morning Esther staggered sleepily into the kitchen rubbing her eyes.

MUCK AGAIN!

'What on earth was going on in the buildings during the night? I could hear an awful lot of bawling.'

'Your dad was up a few times during the night … Rosebud was calving and I think it was a difficult one.'

'Did he have to send for the vet?' asked Esther anxiously.

'No, I think it's all over now … but I can hear him crossing the yard, he'll tell you what went wrong when he comes in. I'll fetch his breakfast, he must be starved.'

Esther looked anxiously in her father's face, but was pleased to see that he was smiling to himself.

'What are you looking so pleased about Dad? I was sure something was dying in the middle of the night.'

'If something didn't die in the night it isn't thanks to the rest of you who slept when one of the cows needed a bit of help to calve … it was left to the old man to sort things out.'

'It was Rosebud wasn't it? Is she all right ?'

Jackson picked up his knife and fork to tackle his eggs and bacon.

'Oh! Come on Dad, tell us how things are. Everything must be OK or else your face would be as long as a fiddle.'

'I don't know where you get such ideas from … I'm always pleasant, it's just that some of the worries of farming can get a chap down from time to time. But you'd better get outside and help Bill with that new milking machine … and … maybe you'll see something that might interest you.'

Esther grabbed her jacket and hurried to the byre wondering what on earth could have pleased her father. The warmth of the cows' breath hit her as she pushed the door open and stepped inside. She hurried over to the small pen where her father always put the newborn calves. She knew it would be a thrill to see the new calf, they were always so beautiful, so very clean! Never in their lives would any newborn farm animal look so pristine and bandbox clean.

'Just you take a look in that pen,' called Bill from the far side of a restless Maud, who could be relied upon to sense any drama on the farm and respond in her usual hysterical way!

Esther stepped over to the pen and looked into the deep fresh straw. She could hardly believe her eyes! Not one calf, not two calves but three little brightly coloured shorthorn calves were snuggled together and dozing happily.

'You're beautiful,' she whispered to the three little heifers. She looked to Rosebud, who was looking a bit uncomfortable but was feeding hungrily, seemingly none the worse for her long delivery.

Esther raced excitedly back to the kitchen where Jackson was studiously reading the morning paper.

'Dad! Dad! You'll have to telephone the Farmers Weekly I've heard that triplets are very rare. They'll probably write an article about them.'

'Calm yourself down Lass. I'll do no such thing, at least, not yet. Few triplets live for more than a few days, there's often a weak one, and that's more than likely after the struggle I had delivering them. There was a dozen legs for me to sort out. I wasn't sure what the hell was in there when she got into difficulty, legs everywhere, back'uns and front'uns all tangled together.'

'You did a very good job, I'm sure they'll all live … in fact I'll look after them and make sure they thrive.'

MUCK AGAIN!

She turned to her smiling mother.

'We'll have to think of some special names for them ... just wait until the neighbours hear about this, you'll get many a free drink in the Grey Mare on the strength of this.

Jackson chuckled as his daughter disappeared to check on their new stock.

'What are you so amused about?" asked Edith happy that today would be one of those red-letter days in farming that none of them would ever forget.

'I was thinking about that sow producing three little pigs and that sneaky hen only managing to lay three eggs ... and then the very animal that was expected to produce only one offspring ... presented us with a litter! That'll keep tongues wagging for a bit in the district! Don't you agree Mother?'

'Yours most of all!" she said to herself as she nodded assent.

6.

COME INTO THE PARLOUR

'**A** what?'

Jackson almost spilled his glass of ale in astonishment.

'Yes, a milking parlour,' repeated Alan Steel. 'I'm thinking of buying one. It's a good idea to be in the forefront of modern technology.'

'In our parlour we drink milk, we never let the cows in to provide it on tap so to speak. Who on earth thought about bringing the cows inside the farmhouse? It must be them new hygienic ideas they're always coming up with in the Farmers Weekly.

Alan laughed gleefully at the old farmer's confusion.

'Tell us more about it Alan,' asked an interested Ben Mossop, a newcomer to the district.

'Aye, you foreigners'll swallow any new daft ideas that the gentlemen farmers bring along.'

'No Jackson, I keep an open mind … and if we can add a few pounds to the monthly milk cheque then I'm all for it.'

'That's right,' agreed Tom Graham thoughtfully, 'I've read about these milking parlours somewhere … maybe there was some talk about such a thing at the Royal Show when we went there last year.'

Jackson nodded.

'That's a likely spot to hear about crackpot ideas, they spend the whole year thinking up new ideas to surprise us all, I suppose the idea of a parlour appeals to the tea-drinking élite in our society.'

MUCK AGAIN!

'Where on earth did you learn a foreign word like élite Jackson?' laughed Alan, 'I thought you went to Bookwell School, not a posh one!'

Jackson sipped his ale very slowly, then nodded his head knowingly.

'Folks like you Alan think that when you walk out of school you leave your brains behind because you've learned all you can. But if I'd done that I wouldn't have had anything in my head to work with. There's a lot of different ways of learning, and it goes on all your life.'

'You're a philosopher as well!'

'Aye, a bit of thinking things out and not just accepting new and unproved ideas that so-called clever men think up, can keep a chap with little education from jumping on every new bandwagon that comes along.'

The conversation in the Grey Mare rose and fell as the farmers discussed this new advertising promotion.

'There's to be a film show at Sandwith next Saturday night when the manufacturers will be showing these parlours at work.'

'Will there be a beer tent?'

'No Jackson, the salesman wants us all to be sober and able to think straight.' Said Alan brightly, 'I'll be there, I've no intention of missing out on something that might bring us dairy farmers into the second half of this century ... we've all been stick-in-the-muds up here for far too long.'

'We're becoming more like ice-cream salesmen with every new idea that comes along. I suppose they'll give us all a white coat to impress the cows! I can't see my best milkers going into a polished gleaming parlour ... they're used to comfort, like being able to lie down and shit at their leisure, not have to move on from pillar to post!'

'I thought you knew nothing about milking parlours Jackson, but you seem to know that cows move into it, then out at the other side,'

'You make the mistake of jumping to conclusions Alan. Us old chaps are capable of reading the farming magazines, but we don't just accept these changes as progress. Think of the loss in milk yield while we're coaxing unwilling cows to step into the parlour! No, it all means a good bit of thought to go into the scheme before we lay out a fortune on what might be a flight of fancy.'

       *   *   *

'Are you going to a funeral Dad?'

'What makes you think that?'

'I never see you polishing your boots unless you're going to a funeral. And it's a Saturday when there's often a burial.'

Jackson lowered his shoe brush in amazement.

'I can look smart without a friend or acquaintance having to die.'

'Yes I know, but it's only on a Thursday when you might polish your boots to go to the auction.'

'Never, I deliberately keep my boots dirty to go there, I don't want to give anybody the idea that they're talking to a gentleman farmer with money to burn.'

'I don't think there's any danger of that,' said Edith as she came into the kitchen carrying the supper tray, ' … you just have to open your mouth and folks will know you're an ordinary chap.'

MUCK AGAIN!

'Well that's put me smartly in my place,' he lowered his boots to the floor.

'It's obvious that you are both dying to know where I'm going tonight.'

'No I'm not Jackson, but you never dress up to go to the pub, so I'm curious to know who deserves this spit and polish.'

Jackson's eyes twinkled.

'Now, now Edith! Wives always think there's another woman in the picture!'

Edith placed the teapot onto the table with a firm thud.

'Don't flatter yourself Jackson, I would love to see you chase another woman ... I just know it wouldn't take long for her to decide to send you back home. A more cantankerous man doesn't live in the district!'

Esther laughed at her mother's spirited observation, even though she knew that she too was curious to know what had inspired her father to spruce himself up.

'I'm going to a lecture ... if you both want to know.'

'A lecture? I didn't know that you'd heard of the word Dad! Are you going to a school or a College?'

'No, I'm going to a farm at Sandwith where they're giving a lecture on milking parlours.'

'What! You are going to buy a milking parlour? I can't believe what I'm hearing Dad! You've hardly accepted the ordinary milking machine, let alone a super building like that! I also know that you've managed to hide a milking stool away in case this modern electricity fails!

'Who have you been talking to Jackson? Lord Lowther? This modern farming is for their Lordships not for the likes of us.'

MUCK AGAIN!

MUCK AGAIN!

'I can't understand my family, one minute they tell me I'm still in the eighteenth century, then the next minute they're complaining that I'm too modern. I don't know what to do to please you. A chap is never right in this house.'

The two women looked at one another, dumb-struck.

'That's given you something to think about, I've never known either of you at a loss for words before.'

He pulled on his shiny boots as he spoke. 'A good farmer has to look ahead and plan for his family, the world won't wait for the stragglers ... is my cheque book in that drawer Edith?'

His wife nodded numbly.

Jackson pocketed the cheques and made for the door. Flash leaped to her feet.

'You needn't bother getting up, you might find yourself out of a job very soon as well, so just get back under the sofa.'

The surprised dog slunk back beside a sleeping Patch. What had happened to her master? Surely this was time to go to the pub? But there was no understanding human beings, they weren't like dogs that have a faultless sense of timing.

'I never thought I'd see the day when our Jackson would be throwing his money about like paper! Fancy him taking a chequebook! I didn't know that he knows how to write a cheque, I always fill them in and he signs them.'

She shook her head incomprehensibly as she cleared the table. The sound of Tom Graham's car pulling away from the farm gate reached their ears.

'He's going with Tom,' said Esther as she peeped through the curtains.

MUCK AGAIN!

'The thing is,' said Edith thoughtfully, 'I thought I always knew what he was thinking … in fact, I've always done most of the thinking for him. Another thing … there's very little money in the bank, so he'd better not write a cheque for more than a hundred pounds or so!'

'You don't have to pay the full amount these days Mam, you just pay a down-payment then you can pay it off so much a month through the bank.'

'It's all too much for me, I rely on the Co-op dividend to pay for my extras.'

'But farming is a business, you have to take risks to move forward and maybe Dad has been given some expert advice, you never know.'

'I know,' retorted Edith hotly, ' … there's no experts in the Grey Mare but it's amazing how many of them become experts after they've downed a few pints. There's nothing new you can tell me about. The silly old fool would be so full of ale that he'd listen to any of his clever cronies … or maybe an expert from Egremont or Whitehaven called into the pub last night.'

'I don't think he would listen to anybody in the pub, he's always telling them what to do. No, he's got the notion from somewhere else. Have you noticed him reading the Farmers Weekly over the last few days? He could have seen those lovely photographs they put in showing all the latest in agriculture.'

'He never takes any notice of anything in the farming magazines, I'm puzzled by it all, it's not like him.'

'Don't worry Mother, once he puts his hand in his pocket he'll think again, he's not used to paying any bills.'

'I wish I could be as sure, they say that men often go through a middle -age difficult time similar to a woman.'

MUCK AGAIN!

'No such thing Mam. Dad hasn't gone through adolescence stage yet, he was born an old man! There's something very fishy about his behaviour, but don't worry. You know, there's a good film on in Egremont tonight, let's go. If the men can go out for the evening so can we, get your hat and coat on, we don't have anybody to take us in a car but a good brisk walk will do us good.'

'But your father might get home before us, with a milking parlour booked for us.'

'A good thing if he sees that we can spend money as well. Come on hurry up or we'll never get there in time for the big picture. Don't feel guilty it's only ninepence each it won't break the bank!'

*   *   *

'You asked that young chap a lot of questions Jackson for somebody who has no intention of buying a milking parlour.'

'Well now Tom who's to say I won't buy a new milking facility as he calls it? An intelligent chap can listen then change his mind, it's no good having set ideas.'

He reached in his inside pocket, '… and to prove it here's my cheque book.'

Tom gazed in amazement, he'd never seen Jackson with such a thing in his hand. The neighbours wouldn't half be surprised if the old man placed an order.

The alert salesman spotted the chequebook and hastened towards this likely customer.

'I see you are interested in improving the quality of your milk sir. I noticed your keen interest throughout my talk.'

MUCK AGAIN!

'Oh yes I've always been at the forefront of agricultural progress young man. Tell me how do I go about having one of these parlours installed in my farmyard?'

The eager salesman grabbed his notebook as a few of Jackson's neighbours idly shuffled closer.

'Surely Jackson isn't going to buy a milking parlour?' said Alan Steel to a farmer standing close to him.

'Why not? I bet he has all sorts of money hidden under his mattress. It's always them that don't seem to have two pennies to rub together who can save up. Today's the first time I've seen him dressed up, he must have a good reason.'

'Your address Sir? I can call next week and assess what changes will need to be made to accommodate a modern facility like the one you have seen on my film.'

'Fine! How about next Thursday lad, any time will do, I'll be around the buildings all day. I have a few ideas of my own as well.'

'Very good Sir. I'm pleased to know that you are giving the idea some thought.'

'Surely you aren't going to install a milking parlour for your cows Jackson? You only have about three that are under ten.'

'Well now Alan, I'm getting on a bit myself so I appreciate the need for comfort. My cows have paid me well for a good many years so it's only right that they should enjoy a bit of luxury in their old age.'

'You weren't talking like that in the Grey Mare last Thursday night. If I remember rightly you were saying that they'd all have nervous breakdowns if they had to learn how to make their way through a milking parlour.'

MUCK AGAIN!

Jackson tapped his walking stick on the barn floor as if to measure what he was going to reply.

'Aye, I did say all that, but I got to thinking and I thought I should look to the future. I have two children at home and Sellafield offers good pay and clean conditions for them to work in. So I was thinking that if I could offer some of these modern working conditions at home then they might stick with it.'

'I never thought you could look that far ahead Jackson!'

'It doesn't do to judge folks too quickly Alan, some times I think about things a bit more deeply than usual ... Aye well! I'm going to have a word with that young chap, I can't let my neighbours get ahead of me in modern methods.'

Jackson went to look for his lift home.

'It looks dark in your kitchen Jackson' noted Tom as he drew his car to a stop at the farm gate.

'I should think Edith'll have gone to bed early, Bill likes to go to a dance and Esther's probably gone to the pictures, they'll come home in the middle of the night!'

'You're only young once Jackson, let them have a good time you never know how hard life can be in the future.'

'True enough, at least they won't have a milking parlour to pay for, they'll have nothing but a life of ease and luxury to look forward to.'

Jackson shouted up the stairs to let Edith know he was home, but there was no answer. He switched on the kitchen light and the sheet of writing paper lying on the bare table immediately caught his eye. He searched in his pocket for his reading glasses to read the note.

Gone to the pictures – will be back late– some leftovers on a plate in the oven.

MUCK AGAIN!

'So much for the excitement of buying a milking parlour!' said Jackson out aloud to himself as he pulled his boots off.

*　　　　*　　　　*

Edith gazed unbelievingly through the window as she watched her husband showing the man around from the milking parlour firm. She couldn't believe all this was happening, but it was true that she didn't understand a lot about the modern farming methods and certainly Jackson had kept them in reasonable comfort in the last few years so it was a matter of trusting his judgement. The two children were pleased, of course, and apparently it had been the sole topic of conversation in the Grey Mare since last Saturday. Nevertheless she felt uneasy about the financial side of it all. They would have to farm well for years and years as far as she could judge. What if Bill and Esther managed to get well-paid jobs at Sellafield? Then Jackson and herself would have to farm into their dotage to meet whatever the payments would work out to be. It was all far too worrying for Edith. She looked out again and saw that the lad was busy writing on a thick writing pad. Jackson was nodding and looking pleased with himself. Oh dear!
She checked the sandwiches and cakes she'd placed out on the kitchen table for the young man. No one ever came to the farm and left without having a bite to eat, no doubt he would discuss what would happen next when they came in. She'd better switch the kettle on again. As she came back into the kitchen she heard the sound of a car driving out of the gate and looked out just in time to catch

the sight of the salesman's car disappearing down the road.

'Why did you let that lad go without bringing him in for a cup of tea and a bite to eat?' she asked Jackson when he came in.

'He didn't have time, he has richer folks to visit. Alan Steel is on his books for later this morning, so I didn't want to keep him back from his job.'

'When are they coming to fit the milking parlour then?' Jackson chuckled to himself as he reached for a beef sandwich.

'When did I say that I was definitely buying a milking parlour?'

'We all thought you were. After all, you asked that young man to call and measure things up!'

'Why not? These salesmen are very quick to assure the buyer that they don't have to commit themselves, when all along they know that the daft farmer has already decided that he's going to buy one even though it lets him in for years of debt. But they like to make out they are doing the selling.'

'That's a dreadful thing to do Jackson when you had no intention of buying the machine.'

'But Edith, just you think what I've learned about this modern machine … and what's more, I've a fair idea how much money Alan Steel and the rest of them will owe to the bank, very interesting!'

'What an awful thing to do! It's deliberately dishonest.'

'At my age I think I can be a bit wicked now and again. You know Edith, I've thoroughly enjoyed it all. It's given them something to talk about in the local pubs. They think they have me weighed up … but far from it … it's always a good thing to keep something up your sleeve! I always say that it's a mistake to make other folks as wise as yourself! '

'You certainly had us guessing. How are you going to explain your change of mind?'

'That's easy! When we discussed the plans, it was clear to me that the layout of this farm is too complicated for such a radical change. Besides, this is a tenancy so any large outlay would benefit the landlord more than us. What you have to remember Edith is that the layout was too complicated, not that I never had a notion of throwing good money away on such a daft modern idea. Just consider what Maud and the rest of them would think about such a change to their routine? It's enough to make animals of their age lose their milk yield as well as the possibility of infertility. The old bull had enough difficulty getting them in-calf, but that young vet wouldn't stand a chance if they had this hassle.'

Edith smiled to herself. She had to admit that a bit of underhand dealing could be more entertaining than the cold truth!

But there again, she long given up the idea of having a husband whose word was his bond.

MUCK AGAIN!

7.

LOVE AND BEAUTY

Esther gasped for breath as she pulled her body the last few painful yards to the cairn on the summit of Scafell Pike. She and her companions in the rambling Club had come the long way up. Starting at Wasdale Head they'd slogged up Sty Head, then to Esk Hause to follow the rocky path towards the huge summit cairn which was tantalising in sight for a half hour or so as they'd struggled over a huge field of boulders which was the last obstacle to cross.

The surge of pleasure which invaded her and the others as they reached the highest peak in England was one which was reserved exclusively for those who tackle the fells.

She and her friend Rose gazed in awe at the view which unfolded below them. To the west the coastal plain lay glittering in the autumn sun and she could see the Irish Sea stretching from there to the horizon.

On the way up she had been reminded almost every step of the way of her father's account of his long walk over to the Langdale valley so many years ago. What a journey it must have been in those days. She would have great pleasure recounting this walk when she reached home tonight.

She looked again towards home and the familiar landmarks, Sellafield with its cooling towers silently working and the farm not far away at Gosforth where she'd been born. A warm sense of belonging to this beautiful County enveloped her, it was uplifting and inspiring. No wonder that Wordsworth had been moved to write his poetry about such places. Surprisingly the words which came immediately into her mind from school days were ....

> 'Earth has not anything to show more fair;
> Dull would he be of soul who could pass by
> A sight so touching in its majesty'

It was surprising as these words were written one early morning upon Westminster Bridge! Surely one of his poems written about the Lakes should have come to mind? But somehow the words had jumped naturally into her consciousness and they certainly captured the moment for her.

She'd often questioned the point of learning sonnets such as this by heart, but now she was aware that all great works of creation are linked on a level which can be reached by various channels; music, literature, painting, Faith and a common love of mankind.

'You look far away!' said Rose smiling at her friend.

'Yes, I was, I thinking about the beauty and majesty up here.'

'It's awesome, look at those mountains below us. I've usually looked up at them when we've taken a car ride up to Wasdale. Now because this is the highest mountain, we can look down on them. It's very majestic! Yes, that's the word I would use too'

The only thing missing is a bit of grass to sit on, it's very much like a lunar landscape,' said Esther who was now ready for her drink and sandwiches. The ramblers had

MUCK AGAIN!

spread themselves out across the large summit area. Some were
delving into their haversacks while others were taking photos.

The two friends settled near the edge where they had a spectacular view of the Wasdale valley and its surrounding fells. Nearby, a man, not in their group, was sitting with his Border collie dog beside him enjoying the view and his snack.

'Just look at those two,' said Rose nodding in the their direction.

'What is there to see?'

'Well, the man is obviously enjoying the scenery and his dog seems to be enjoying it as well. Look! As the owner moves his head around, the dog seems to be doing the exact same thing, tell me, you live on a farm with dogs … can they enjoy a lovely view?'

Esther laughed.

'I'm no dog psychiatrist! You should ask my dad, he seems to know what goes on in animals' heads. But yes, the dog does seem to be watching something, but maybe he can see the sheep grazing down below. Dad reckons it's all smells with animals so maybe he's sniffing things we can't smell. But dogs have a way of looking happy with their tongues hanging out like that, but why they are happy is anybody's guess.'

Soon they set off down towards Wasdale and Esther learned that the way down can be as equally hard as the slog up!

'Oh Dad, you don't know how lucky you were to have worked up at Wasdale Head when you were a young man.'

'Aye, it was hard work tramping about to find straying sheep and the farmer had little to pay us and very little to feed us on.'

'Oh but wasn't it lovely to go to the top of Scafell and see the view?"

'What would I want to go trekking up to them big draughty summits for? What do you think we kept dogs for?'

'What do you mean?'

'If you'd looked closely at the mountains you would have noticed that the design was very clever, your mother would say that it was designed by a master hand. But whoever thought it out had shepherds in mind. Now if you looked closely you would see that there are a good few passes which allow folks to walk through from one valley to the other.'

'Yes, like Sty Head.'

'That's right, nobody in their right mind is going to walk up to those wild and barren summits for no good reason. All you have to do is stand at the top of a Pass and send the dogs up higher and they'll fetch the sheep down. That's good and sensible farming.'

'But the views from the top are terrific, did you not think it was all very beautiful and weren't you tempted go up higher to get a better view?'

'Only a few times, if the dog didn't come back quickly. Things always go wrong up there when it's blowing a gale or when the snow's drifting and hiding the sheep. It might look lovely but the wet snow seeping into you boots and melting to run down your back can soon spoil the romantic view. Remember we didn't have the expensive waterproofs that you see the walkers wearing nowadays.

They work somewhere else and can afford to buy the best of walking gear.'

'I suppose so,'

'You're very good at dampening the lass's enthusiasm Jackson. I think she has a lovely hobby that gets her out among different folks and lets her see how beautiful this county is.'

'And when we came down we went into the hotel and looked at the photos of the early climbers who didn't have the modern clothes either.'

'But they had a choice about where they went and how they spent their leisure time, but for the likes of us it was a way of earning a poor living. But I've got to admit that I thought about nowt else when I was in school except the day I could leave and go off up the fells to learn how be a shepherd.'

'Well, like I was saying Dad, we were talking in the bar about the herdwick sheep being hefted, the townsfolk from Whitehaven had never heard about the sheep being trained over many generations to stay on their own patch of fellside. It's a very clever idea, the old farmers certainly worked things out to save the flocks getting muddled and save themselves from having to walk from valley to valley looking for lost sheep.'

'Esther you've got to remember that all this cleverness in farming whether it's up in the fells or on the flat plains is the result of poverty. In times gone by it was survive or starve so as a breed we became clever. It was the farmers who fed this country during the war, Churchill knew he was onto a winner when he asked us for help.'

'You're talking the way your mouth stands again!' snapped Edith who was no disciple of the wartime leader,

'he had no choice either, but he had the knack of making us think that anything that was successful was his idea.'
Jackson ignored his wife's remark, he was used to her strong religious or socialist ideas.
'What are you smiling at Dad?'
Esther knew from experience that her father was recalling some funny incident from years ago.
'When you talk about hefted sheep made me think of something that happened up Wasdale a few years back.'
'I hope you're not going to malign those hard-working farmers Jackson.'
'What! me? I always tell the truth. There's nothing funnier than the truth, that's why I stick to it.'
'Go on Dad let's hear it.'
'Well, Alan who farmed up there then, was busy gathering the tups from the fells, around the New Year it was. They had finished serving the ewes and he was gathering them and putting them into a field near the farm so that he could sort them out and sell the old useless ones. He had gathered in forty-eight of his forty-nine rams and was searching the fellside for the missing one. Well … he was well up Black Sail Pass when he spotted it going over Windy Gap following a ewe that must have been missed in the courtship stakes. Anyway, Alan was tired and as it was getting late he decided to let it get on with what it was supposed to do. He thought it would make its way back to the rest of the flock later on. It was a waste of his time sending the dogs on such a long run.'
He paused for the maximum effect and said smartly to Edith, ' … put a bit of coal on that fire Edith it can be real cold up Black Sail!'

MUCK AGAIN!

Esther laughed.

'Did the ram find its way home?'

'If you believe all you hear about hefted sheep then it should have rushed back home after the honeymoon.'

'But it didn't?'

'Didn't they tell you about the pop marks they put on the sheep so that every sheep can be identified if they wander off?'

Esther shook her head.

'No, the ram couldn't be found anywhere on its own patch. As Alan was planning to fatten it and sell it in the auction and didn't want to take a big load, then have to take one ram on its own.'

'Why did he have to sell it? He could have sold the others, surely one sheep doesn't make much difference?'

'You don't know much about sheep for a farmer's daughter.'

'Well we only winter a few here, they don't interest me very much.'

'The ram was old and had worn its teeth down so he planned to fatten it up while it could still chew.'

'I see, did it ever come home?'

'Well, it was like this, Alan was in the auction in Cockermouth looking for new rams when he met a farmer from the top of Buttermere valley who collared him as soon as he arrived saying that Alan's old ram had come down to his farm with his ewes. He said he didn't want it with a set of teeth like that.'

'Then set the dogs on it and drive it back to Wasdale,' Alan said.

'I've tried that but the dogs are weary of chasing it, the daft thing comes back to my ewes each time we try, it can find its way back faster than the dogs do, you can bloody well send a trailer round … I don't want it eating my winter grass.'

'Did he send a trailer?'

'Aye he did, because you don't want ill-feeling between farmers so he asked a friend over there to fetch it to Wasdale the next time he came that way. Alan was lucky because the lost ram landed home the next week.'

'So that's the end of the tale?'

'No it isn't. The very next morning Alan went to check his rams and the old toothless one had managed to find a small hole in the fence and had worked away at it during the night, and in spite of its lack of teeth, had managed to chew through the fence and then disappeared. They couldn't find it anywhere, but a postcard arrived a few days later from Buttermere saying that Alan had deliberately let the ram go back over there!'

Esther laughed. 'What did he do?'

He said that two could play at that game, so he sent a postcard to Buttermere with a brief note …

'My tup is attracted to one of your ewes. It must be true love. So keep the bugger'.

8.

GHOSTS AND THINGS

The storm lashed relentlessly against the kitchen window as Jackson and his family sat reading on this wild winter's night.

'I hope the slates don't blow off the roof,' said Edith uneasily; she didn't like the strength of the wind.

'Have you heard anything blowing down into the yard?"

'No, I haven't.'

'Well what are you fussing about? There's no need to anticipate disasters before they happen. Wait until you hear something then start to worry.'

'It's all right for you Jackson you never seem to bother yourself about anything.'

'Well we are only tenant farmers so it's the landlord's worry not ours.'

'Isn't it? I seem to remember that in the terms of the tenancy we have to maintain the buildings in a reasonable order.'

'Does it? Well then, if anything flies off we'll put it back when the gale dies down. Does it say anything in the tenancy about acts of God? I thought we were only liable for reasonable wear and tear of farming life that we have caused ourselves, not for the act of a revengeful God.'

'I think God has a fair idea of who needs punishment. You should watch your language and tell a few less lies.'

'Leave Dad alone Mam, he's not answerable for the weather. I should think this destructive sort of weather is maybe sent by the devil. I mean, if you're so sure that there's a God then it's logical to think there's a devil.'

'Quite right Esther, I'm sure there's a devil somewhere who constantly tempts us.'

Jackson put down his copy of the Geographical Magazine having decided that it was time he controlled the conversation.

'I've been reading about that sort of thing here in this magazine. They still have witch doctors in Africa and they reckon that they're as successful as the proper doctors.'

'It depends what's wrong with you if you ask me. There might be something to be said for consulting a witch doctor if you have mental or emotional trouble, but if you have a need for surgery then it's a different story.'

'Maybe, but I've also read that the witch doctor can cast a spell on your enemy by sticking pins in a model of him. Often the enemy wastes away and dies.'

Esther shivered at the thought.

'I suppose the thinking behind that is that you should love one another which is a Christian ethic.'

'That must have made it easier for the missionaries when a lot of the work had been done for them.'

'I don't think so Dad, in some of those places they cooked and ate the missionaries, it can't have been that easy for them.'

'I bet they were a dry lot to eat! I fall asleep if I have to go to church and listen to them, so I have a lot of respect for anybody who managed to get worked up enough to eat them.'

'They are savages who know no better Jackson. Those of us who live in decent Christian countries know better than to believe that sort of rubbish.'

MUCK AGAIN!

'But you know Edith, I always have a strong feeling that your May might have a model of me and maybe a few others with pins sticking in them.'
Esther laughed out aloud.
'There's nothing funny about such an ignorant remark. Our May is a God-fearing woman.'
'Aye, I should think there are times when God fears her! I know I do. Come on Esther, admit that she puts the fear of God into you.'
'I have to agree. You never know what she's going to consider is shocking. By the way Mam, how is she getting on with courting with the vicar?'
'Now there's a chap I can admire! Anybody who fancies getting into bed with May wouldn't have any problems with a few cannibals!'
'Don't talk like that Jackson I'm sure he will treat her with the greatest of respect.'
'That sounds dull, doesn't it Esther?'
'Don't you involve me in your discussion, all I know is that she can freeze me to my seat when she turns her gaze and shakes her earrings in my direction. I'm always scared that a careless remark could set me on the road to Hell … to her way of thinking.'
'Exactly! That's what I'm trying to say. She makes me feel guilty when I'm sure I've done nothing wrong.'
'I should think you've always done something wrong so she might be right Dad.'
A gust of wind suddenly buffeted the window and Edith glanced uneasily through the curtains.
'Esther you should go outside and check the buildings in case there's any damage. Your father's a bit too old to go out in this storm.'

MUCK AGAIN!

Esther shook her head.

'Sorry Mam, but it's too spooky to wander about in the dark at this time of the night. I'm too scared to go into the barns. Another thing, I don't like disturbing the rats, they'll be running around out looking for feed. No, I'll just wait until the morning.'

'You're no better than those superstitious natives of Africa!'

Jackson laughed.

'You know Edith, it's not only the ignorant natives of darkest Africa who are easily frightened in the dark. I can think of situations nearer home where so-called religious folks were scared out of their wits by what they thought was a ghost.'

'Oh! When was that?'

'Can you remember me telling you about the time I went over to the Grasmere area with Jimmy Marshall?'

'Yes, I remember.'

Jackson settled himself more comfortably in his chair close by the fire while his wife and daughter pulled theirs nearer to his.

'You know how I said that the folks who live up them valleys are very superstitious compared with the likes of us who live over here?"

They both nodded.

'I think it's because they've been isolated up in them remote valleys for generations so they're easily frightened.'

Edith snorted her disagreement.

'It's true Edith, they still expect to see boggles and ghosts coming down from the tops of the fells just like their ancestors did. Remember how scared Jimmy was when we came down Rossett Ghyll? He was scared of seeing the ghost of the old peddler woman who'd been found dead up there. Lots of folks swear they've seen her ghost wandering along the path. Up yonder, just as in deepest Africa they cling on to their pagan ideas.'

Edith laughed, scorning at the idea.

'You needn't laugh. Just you invite one of your relatives over there to take a walk up a mountain after dark and you'll soon know if they're scared or not.'

'Well get on with your story, then we'll judge the truth of it all.'

'Jimmy's family were very religious and one Sunday evening they went up to the church at Chapel Stile. Jimmy always helped to work the bellows that kept the organ going, so he thought I'd like to help him. It was hard work because if you didn't keep it going the organ would slow down and short notes would whine and drone. Of course that particular night the vicar had chosen the fastest hymns he could, he said that when there were two strong young men there to keep things going he'd choose some brisk hymns. Everything was going fine apart from a few of the older fatter folks sitting at the front. The lively pace had one or two of the plumper women mopping their brows and gasping for breath. The devil must have been in Jimmy because he speeded things up so much that the thin miserable woman who was playing the organ was also gasping for breath and desperately signalling Jimmy to slow down. It was so funny that I was choking with laughter, the old church seemed to rock with the vibration.'

Jackson burst into laughter as he remembered that night so many years ago. Edith, who had picked up her darning, tried not to smile as Esther joined in her father's hilarity.

'Is that the end of the tale Dad?"

'Oh no, … the last hymn was Onward Christian Soldiers and Jimmy decided to sit in the front pew … leaving me to pump the organ alone. To start with things went well, the congregation had rested while the vicar had said some prayers so they were all ready to march to war! After the first two verses I felt my arms aching like mad. Things began to slow down, and then slow down a bit more. I glared at Jimmy who was sitting like an angel close to a big fat farmer who could snort like a bull. As I slowed down the organist had to skip notes to keep up with the congregation who were racing away faster and faster. Eventually she gave up and let them scamper to the final line on their own. Of course, by now Jimmy was nearly wetting himself as he watched my struggle. The organist and me both staggered out of the church while the locals congratulated themselves on the great hymn singing and invited me to come anytime to enjoy their music. I swore I'd never set foot in there again. Of course the bold Jimmy had enjoyed every minute of it all!'

'I can't see anything pagan about all that Jackson, except your merriment in the Lord's house.'

'That's the point I'm coming to. We set off, Jimmy and his Aunt Mary and me to walk back to his house. We had a storm lantern to show the way along the road that was pitch black. I must admit that once we'd left the cottages behind, the darkness wrapped round us like a blanket and the wind began to whip up a bit. The lamp blew out about five times or so before we gave up the idea of using it at all. Once the light had gone we could see a little better, but only a little. Sounds in the darkness seem to be much louder and threatening than during the daylight, the becks tumbling down the fellside seemed too ready to crash on top of us. The minute our feet s plash into water we were sure we'd stepped off the road and were on the point of slipping down a grassy slope. I'll admit it was a bit frightening for a young daft chap.'

'I'm scared just listening Dad!'

Edith got up to brew a cup of tea.

'Seeing you don't believe all this Edith I'll carry on telling Esther about it.'

He chuckled as Edith said she'd rather hear every word, as no doubt it was as true as it was likely to be considering who was telling the tale!

'I don't care whether it's all true or not it promises to be good story.'

Jackson pulled his chair closer to the fire and the two women did the same. Edith picked up her darning to occupy her as she listened to the rest of the tale.

'Sitting here in the warmth with a good light makes it hard to imagine what it was like almost feeling your way along that road. Every now and again a cloud would blow over and it was comforting to see the road ahead, then when it went black again we tried to remember which way the road bent. It was pretty quiet, we could hear each other breathing and we knew that Jimmy's mother was scared because her breathing was very rapid. Then we all became aware of a tiny light away up the hillside ahead of us. It looked like somebody repeatedly striking a match and letting it go out then striking it again.'

'Maybe it was somebody coming the other way?'

'Let your father tell his story.'

MUCK AGAIN!

'It very was spooky and Mrs Marshall was scared to death. It's Old Nick! It's Old Nick! She kept saying. You know Esther, they say there's boggles and ghosts that haunt the old slate quarries, sometimes the men won't go to work if they think there's a bad omen! I must say I was feeling scared by this time, I kept thinking about the way we'd laughed and joked in church. We would have no protection against any evil spirit. I knew Jimmy was thinking the same thing because in spite of the darkness I could see his pale face.'

'What about the flashes of light?'

'They were coming nearer and nearer to us; and in addition there was a sharp thumping sound as well. Jimmy was scared to death and was all for running back to Chapel Stile and the safety of the village. But I said no because nobody would believe us, maybe it would be better if we hid behind a big rock and kept as quiet as we could until the scary thumping and flashing had passed. 'Yes' agreed Jimmy's Aunt 'I think that's a good idea, look! there's a big rock up on our right, we must keep absolutely quiet and pray as hard as we can.'

Believe me I've never prayed as hard in my life as I did that night! In the daylight everything is sensible but up in them lonely valleys in the pitch black, you're ready to believe anything.'

He handed his mug to Esther.

'Fill that up Lass will you? It's thirsty work talking; I don't know how you women manage it.'

'You've had as much practice talking as any woman,' said Edith tartly. 'Somehow a pint of ale can make your tongue wag non-stop.'

MUCK AGAIN!

'How do you know? I've never seen you cross the threshold of a pub!'

'Neither of us fancy making fools of ourselves in the pubs Jackson, but I know what's said! You can't tell me that they all tell me lies … most of what they tell me must be right.'

'It's a terrible thing when you can't have a quiet drink without looking out for spies sitting in some dark corner.'

'Mam doesn't need any spies, your voice can be heard by folks sitting outside, especially in summer.'

'That's beer talking Esther, I only hope that decent people take no notice.'

'Come on Dad tell us what the devil looks like … nobody's listening outside this window!'

'It would serve you right if I forgot what happened next. Like I always say, it's the true tales that are the best.'

'Go on then Dad, we're listening.'

'Like I said, we hid behind this big rock that overlooked the road … and waited. I could feel Jimmy shaking close to me and Mrs Marshall's eyes were tight shut while her lips were moving in silent prayer. The thumping and sparking were now quite close. We kept as still as statues as the sparks drew close and flashed against the shiny wet rock. I decided to peep over the edge of the rock as I guessed the devil or whatever it was would be past us by now. So I raised my head and looked below. You'll never guess what I saw!'

Jackson paused to keep his listeners guessing; he wasn't a popular storyteller in most of the pubs in the district for nothing!

'What did you see?' said an exasperated Esther.

MUCK AGAIN!

'Believe it or not, I was looking down on a big Clydesdale mare who was making her way to the village!'

'What was the sparking then? I can understand the thumping of her feet.'

'The old mare had decided that home was the place for her and had broken through a wire fence. A piece of wire had stuck in one of her shoes and it sparked as her big heavy foot struck the metalled road surface. If she'd walked on the grass there wouldn't have been any sparking at all, nor would we have heard any thumping!'

'That's a great story Dad, I enjoyed it.'

'What about you then Edith? Plenty of your relatives live over there. Just ask them about what you can bump into up in them fells.'

'My relatives have a bit more sense than to believe any pagan nonsense!'

'Everybody says that ... until they're asked to check the dark barns or walk through a thick wood on a black, windy night. How about checking them triplets Esther, they're maybe scared to death in their dark pen!'

'Are you ever frightened of anything Dad?'

'Only your Aunt May! I would defy any boggle to face her on a dark night!'

'Go on Dad she's not as bad as all that!'

' ... or even face her on a fine Sunday afternoon' he said to himself.

MUCK AGAIN!

9.

A LITTLE TROUBLE

Jackson walked contentedly behind his long string of milking cows which stretched a good way ahead of him. He was taking them to the station field, which was a fair walk for them, but in summertime they could graze a more distant field and get back home before it grew dark. In the distance he could just see Mollie, the friendliest of his cows turning the last corner before they reached the field. She's at least five lengths ahead of any of the others, he said aloud. Mollie was always looking for cars, bikes or anything human to stop and gaze at with her big liquid eyes.

Patch glanced up expectantly when he heard his master speak, but no, there was no command. He had hoped there would be because he was weary of trailing behind the slow feet of the last cow.

Suddenly things began to liven up. Jackson had left the field gate open yesterday afternoon so that the first cows could make their own way into the field without having to hang about on the road. The cows were now disappearing round the last corner at a rate of knots. Soon only Jackson and an excited Patch were left to turn the corner. There must be something going on in the field thought Jackson to make this lazy lot gallop like that.

He knew that most of the herd wouldn't have the remotest idea why they were dashing along, being herding animals they simply copied the leading cow, and Mollie had a curiosity that was unmatched in the district. Maybe somebody had dumped an old bike in the field; that would be enough to have Mollie behaving like a bull in a Spanish bullring. She loved to hook her horns round any interesting piece of rubbish and try to toss it in the air.

When man and dog reached the field gate they were astonished to see the herd racing across the cliff top that overlooked the station. Even the old matrons with swinging udders had joined in the chase. 'I'm glad they've been milked' he said to Patch, 'otherwise we'd be milking butter.' Patch shook his ears in agreement, whatever his master was saying reflected the mood of the whole thing.

Jackson's eyes searched the far corner of the field to see what they were heading for. To his surprise he spotted a little black Shetland pony racing ahead of the sprightly Mollie with reins and stirrups flying loosely as he galloped.

Patch itched to join the chase but had to rock expectantly on his paws, a greyhound held back in the traps, couldn't have been more ready.

Suddenly Jackson whistled Patch to cut off the cows' attack and swiftly and expertly the herd was diverted away from the piste of the beleaguered pony which galloped towards the gate intent on making its escape. Jackson stood in the gateway and collected the small animal as it made a dash for the open road.

He examined it closely taking in the smart bridle and soft felt saddle, obviously a child's pony that must have shed its rider the day before and continued its outing alone. She had probably spent the night in the station field. Jackson fastened the gate as the curious cows returned to view their quarry, but as Patch was eyeing them threateningly through the bars of the gate, they approached with due care. The journey back home was slower because Jackson couldn't ride the bike and lead the pony.

As soon as he entered the yard he tied the black Shetland to the Dutch barn gate and took its saddle off to make it a bit more comfortable.

As he walked behind the pony on his way to hang the saddle in the stable he was suddenly struck a resounding blow on his back.

'Good God! The little bugger's kicked me … with both back feet.'

He made his way to the stable and was just coming out when Esther appeared at the kitchen door.

'What a lovely little pony, where did you find her?'

She was in the station field this morning, she's run away from some kiddie. But watch her' he warned as Esther was about to touch the pony.

'She's done her best to break my back, she had a go with both back feet.'

'She'll be frightened, that's all. She needs a bit of kindness.'

'She's not a bit frightened. Just look at her, she's as calm as a cucumber. I reckon she's been spoilt and is used to getting her own way. Just fetch me one of them fancy halters you have for leading the calves on the show field. It'll make her feel more comfortable after spending the night with her bridle on.'

Esther hurried to find the halter then handed it to her father.

'Now Lass, we'll tie her up to the wheel of the cart near the wall so that anybody passing by will notice her and may know whose pony she is. We'll make sure there's not much room between her and the wall so that she can't turn round and kick us as we approach her. She's only little but she can catch us unaware, and by God, she can pack a punch, I can feel my back after that attack, I'm thankful that she didn't kick me in the ribs it's enough to break a couple.'

'Don't exaggerate Dad, she's no bigger than a calf.'

'You can look after her from now on, because I'm likely to kick her back if she tries it on again. Anyhow we'd better go inside for a cup of coffee before the day's work starts.'

'She kicked you!' said Edith when Jackson reached that point in the story. 'What did you do to her?'

'It seems I'm guilty before my case is heard. That's exactly what our Esther said, as though I know nothing about how to handle a daft pony!'

'Well, most ponies behave themselves, especially if a child rides them.'

'That's right Mam,' said Esther 'she must be a danger to whoever owns her. She's probably hungry so I'll feed her when I go back out.'

'You needn't bother Esther, she's already too fat, it's a wonder a little kiddie can sit astride her, no wonder he or she has fallen off. The best you can do Esther is to put her into that top hull, give her a bucket of water and leave her there until tomorrow morning, by that time somebody will have called to see if we have her.'

'Right! Dad, I'll do as you say. I'll just have a read of the paper for a few minutes.'

'I didn't know you ever read the paper!'

MUCK AGAIN!

'I'm looking in the Whitehaven News to see if there's a dance in the Market Hall next Saturday. I think I'd enjoy a night out at a dance Dad.'

'But you're already spending every Sunday rambling and scrambling over the roughest fells you can find! You'll have no energy left to do a decent day's work.'

'Ignore him Esther … I remember a time when he didn't know what time of night it was when he came in from the pub.'

'I'm off to put that pony into the hull, I'll be sure to leave the top half of the door open, she's probably used to a smart stable. There's already some clean bedding in there, so she can lie down if she wants to.'

'You'd think she was a show jumper or something! She seems to me to have been spoilt enough and needs a bit of starving and proper exercise.'

Esther left the kitchen, then a couple of minutes later ran back in.

'The pony Dad, she's gone, she's broken her halter and disappeared.

'She can't have gone far,' he reached for his cap and stood up.

'Good God! My back is sore, she's more trouble than both Clydesdales put together. The smaller the horse or pony, the more awkward they can be. Added to that … she's a mare, and it's well known that the female of any species is troublesome. She's more work than she's worth if you ask me. We'll have to catch her and that's going to be a hard enough job, but my daughter who thinks I frighten the pony can have the job of bringing her back into the yard. It'd be a good idea to open the gate and let

MUCK AGAIN!

her take her chance with the traffic. Anyway, I'd better go out to see what's going on.'

'Be careful Esther, I don't want you injured when it's not even our animal.'

'That's good! When it was me who got kicked it was my own fault, but if it's Esther it's suddenly the pony's fault!'

'Get yourself out there Jackson and help the lass.'

'Look Dad, there she is, at the bottom of the paddock,' she pointed to the little black pony that was grazing happily in the far corner of the small field minus her halter.

Patch and Flash were standing at the open gate weighing up the situation. They were used to rounding up sheep or cows that were often in this paddock. Esther glanced at them.

'Couldn't we round her up with the dogs, they look as though they are ready to have a go.'

'Not likely, she's capable of kicking the living daylights out of them if they get near her hooves. Unless you can lasso her you'd better fetch a couple of halters, one each, then you can go and try to catch her with a handful of sweets while I wait here in case she makes dash for this open gate.'

Esther collected the halters and the sweets then made her way towards the pony speaking gently and holding out her hand with the titbits. The pony looked up and watched her closely as she approached, but she didn't move a foot, allowing the girl to get up close to her. She sniffed the offered hand and just as Esther was about to put the long rope of the halter over her neck, she dashed off at a speed that wouldn't disgrace a steeplechaser. Esther hurried after her while the two dogs whined with impatience, they were sure they could sort the silly animal out, after all, she wasn't even part of a herd! Why was there so much trouble with this single, tiny sort of cow?

'Sit still!' said Jackson, aware of the dogs' anxiety, 'wait a bit longer, I want to see which one of these two women will win in the end. I'd put my shirt on the little pony!'

Esther's breath was running out as the two of them raced round the field. The pony was obviously enjoying this game with a new friend. She lowered her head and kicked her feet in the air a few times, she didn't seem to tire.

Then Jackson took pity on his daughter and let the dogs sort things out. The dogs divided to surround the stubborn pony and bring her back to the farmyard.

Jackson could see the shock in the pony's eyes as the racing dogs streaked towards her, but the shock was quickly overtaken by her escape mechanism.

She took off, heels flashing intent on reaching the safety of the open gate. She passed Jackson as though she was winning the three-thirty at Carlisle by a good six lengths. Not knowing her way she was soon trapped in the corner between the byre door and the turnip shed.

The two dogs drew to a sliding, panting halt beside Jackson. Now it was their turn to have shocked looks on their faces, they'd never had to round up a cow that could gallop as fast as this one across the paddock.

They would certainly have to keep a close eye on such a tricky addition to the farm.

Fed up with the dance the pony had led them Jackson pushed her smartly against the wall to put the halter on her.

'I think it's time this daftness is over Esther, look at her, she's enjoyed every minute of it. She's used to leading some poor kid a right song and dance if you ask me. Take her over to the cart and tie her up tightly with her nose close to the wheel where she can't see what's going on behind her. I'll fetch my pinchers and take her shoes off, then if she does kick anybody she won't do as much damage as she might, then you can put her into that empty hull. Think on, let her go hungry until tomorrow, she's far too fat.'

'Goodness knows how fast she'll be able to gallop if she ever loses weight! If she stays here for a few days you'll have to teach her a few manners.'

'Me? Why me?'

'I'm not having a wilful animal on this farm, the rest of the stock would soon get ideas about who is in charge. Besides, if anybody saw me riding around on a pony as tiny as this one they'd report me to that cruelty society your mother was talking about, remember Charlie? He was nothing but a nuisance, I was glad when he went back to Whitehaven and his ice-cream round. I was told that even there he used to bolt down the street, it's a wonder he didn't kill or injure any children.'

Esther nodded remembering the troublesome Charlie.

'I hope the owner comes to collect her soon.'

The next morning as they finished breakfast Esther said that she was dying to try riding the black pony.

'Don't put a saddle on her, just try her out bareback for a start.'

'Why's that Dad?'

'Just do as I say, you'll probably be able to tell me why a bit later on today … don't let her get her head down to graze she can do that tonight when we leave her in the paddock for the night with the milking cows.'

MUCK AGAIN!

Esther disappeared in the direction of the hull.

'Will she be all right with the cows Jackson remember they did chase her in the station field.'

'It'll do her the world of good to share the field with the cows, they'll soon lose interest and she'll be so hungry she'll graze without causing any more trouble.'

The next morning as the cows lined up to enter the byre to be milked, the little black pony joined them. She was nuzzled along by the protective Mollie. She attempted to kick out at the fussy cow, but she was pushed along quickly by the rest of the herd. Jackson had been expecting this and collected her easily, but was so busy that he decided to tie her up in the adjoining barn until he could attend to her.

At twelve o'clock as Jackson was sitting waiting for Edith to serve his dinner, Esther came in.

'What's wrong with you lass? You don't usually look so dirty, have you been cleaning out the pigsties like I asked you to do yesterday.'

'No Dad, I've been riding … if you can call it that!'

'What's wrong, she's only a little bit of a pony.'

Jackson was chuckling quietly to himself.

'I know now why you said I should leave the saddle in the stable. The first thing she did was to roll in the first bit of soft ground we came to.'

'You mean to say she waited until you'd passed the midden? That's a favourite spot for them little ponies to have a roll. Keep her on a hard road or a stony path.'

'She's so near to the ground that she's down before you know about it, Clydesdales have a bit of height so you can jump off in good time.'

MUCK AGAIN!

'Aye, a decent sized horse is much better to handle in every way, but folks choose a Shetland for their kids to ride because they reckon it's less dangerous than falling from a bigger animal, but they can be trapped easily especially if they have their feet in stirrups.'

'She's got an 'O' level in bucking, but she only threw me a couple of times. I soon spotted the signs. She's also excellent at moving through to a decent gallop then stopping dead while I sail on!'

Jackson was obviously enjoying his daughter's discomfort.

'Don't smile like that Dad, you knew what to expect but I didn't.'

'Has she kicked you yet?'

'I thought she was going to have a go at me with her front feet but I moved away kind of sharpish, but I can't imagine her kicking with her front feet.'

'Believe me, she's probably had practice doing that as well.'

'Can she be cured?"

'It'll take a lot of patience, but we don't have the time to spend on an animal that doesn't bring any money onto the farm. What else did she do?'

'I'd just ridden her to the far end of the paddock when a rabbit popped out of the dyke … and she bolted, I was more surprised than the rabbit as I picked myself up.'

'I should think she's just about exhausted her repertoire in one morning! Is she limping and dirty as well?'

'She's dirty, but she's not damaged in any way. I've left her cooling her heels in the hull.'

MUCK AGAIN!

'It's all new to me, the farm horses don't get down and roll about in the muck, nor do they decide to bolt in the middle of a day's work.'

'When they're very young they try all sorts on, but it's a question of good training, just like dogs or any working animal. Somebody has ruined a smart little pony. It's a pity because the little thing is in charge of things and nobody gets any pleasure from her.'

*   *   *   *   *

The following Sunday morning Edith opened the door to the rare knock to find a tall, distinguished looking gentleman standing on the step.

'I'm looking for our Shetland pony and I'm told she's here.'

'My husband's in the byre over there,' she indicated the door, 'just go in, he'll be pleased to see you.'

'Jim Brodie,' the visitor said as he shook hands with Jackson. 'I understand you found my pony. Thank you for taking her in and looking after her.'

'How did you come to lose her?'

'To be honest with you Mr Strong, she is a very difficult pony, she throws my daughter off and then bolts. Somehow I think we've made some mistakes. You see, we bought Trigger when she was little more than a foal, we thought it would be a good idea if Sheena and the pony learned together.'

Jackson laughed.

'Then you discovered that the pony did all the learning and your daughter soon lost control of her.'

'How did you know?'

'When I was a young chap I spent as much time as I could helping in the stables of some of the gentry around here. I learned as much as I could about riding and handling light horses, mostly hunters and carriage horses. But small ponies were always kept for the children of the house to ride and for light trap and carting work. They were often more trouble to handle than the bigger more expensive horses. We had to sort out any problems because their children had to have safe mounts, not like our kids who have to learn by bad experiences.'

'I'm not sure what you do about things because my daughter is now afraid of her.'

'I notice you called her after that cowboy Roy Roger's horse, well it might be of some comfort to you to know that even Rogers would likely have problems with your Trigger!'

Jim Brodie laughed.

'I must say that's a great comfort, what do you think I should do Mr Strong? Could you train her for me? I'd pay you well.'

'No lad, I'm too busy. My daughter Esther, she's over there milking, has been sorting her out a bit, but whether she'd agree to help I don't know.'

Jim looked down the row of cows where he could see Esther working, she obviously couldn't hear the conversation above the clatter of the milking machine and the milk tins.

'But she's an adult, isn't it cruel for a small pony to be ridden by an adult? She's too heavy.'

'I know the pony is tiny, but a Shetland is built a bit like a donkey. You'll have seen photos of donkeys carrying loads much bigger than themselves? It looks cruel, but some of these little breeds are sturdy and would never have survived unless they could earn their keep. Ponies and horses need work if they're to remain healthy, yours is too fat and is in danger of suffering from laminitis if you're not careful. '

'What's laminitis?'

'It's a very painful condition of the feet which the direct result of a pony becoming too fat. Lack of exercise and overfeeding is true neglect and more cruel than a sharp touch of a riding whip which directs the pony's mind towards what it should be doing.'

'Do you think your daughter would help us?'

'She leads a busy life, but I'll ask her tonight after she's been for her hill walk. How do you intend to get your pony home?'

'My daughter is too nervous to ride her so I'll have to lead Trigger back to Egremont. I'll come and see you tomorrow evening if that's all right with you Mr Strong, by then your daughter may have decided to take Trigger on. If she doesn't perhaps you could us what to do about the pony.'

'Fine, we'll see you then.'

*   *   **   *

Esther listened closely to what her father said about the visit of Mr Brodie as they sat at the supper table that evening.

'You can earn yourself a bit of handy pocket money if you take the pony on Lass, but it'll take time and patience, neither of which you have at this time of the year, but it's up to you.'

Esther considered the proposition for a few minutes then answered her father.

'You didn't give him the idea that I might take on his pony?'

'No, because I think it's too much for a busy person to cope with.'

'I'm going to say no because I'd have keep asking you what to do and I'd have to teach his daughter how to handle the pony. Besides, what if Trigger went back to her old ways as soon as she got home. Then if she harmed Sheena it would be my fault. No, folks should find out all about riding and looking after a pony before they buy one.'

'Good,' said her mother, 'I'm glad you have enough sense to know when things are too complicated.'

'Right I'll tell Jim Brodie when he comes tomorrow.'

'Didn't he asked for advice if Esther said no?'

'He did, the best thing for him would be to sell the daft thing, but it's not fair to sell her unless he warns a buyer that she is a danger to a child. The best thing would be for him to send both the little girl and the pony to a riding school for lessons, it'll cost him a fair bit, but it's his own fault.'

'I'm very impressed by the way you've broken-in and trained all our horses so well Dad.'

Jackson laughed.

'It's a right state of affairs when a lost pony has to invade our farm before my own daughter realises what good things go on here, right under her nose!'

10.

BAD HABITS

'**D**ad, you should give up chewing that horrible black twist, tobacco is very bad for you,' said Esther as they leaned over the paddock gate. Her father had expertly sent a stream of brown liquid towards a white hen that had wandered a bit too close to danger. The hen was still white but with unusual streaks of brown on her feathers.

'And, what did that hen do to you? the poor thing looks a right mess. If anybody comes into this yard they'll think you've bought yet one more unusual animal. They all know that you'll snap up anything out of the ordinary that comes onto the market. Remember that Dexter cow? Folks came from miles around to have a look at her, but she was only a nuisance, like Charlie and that little Shetland pony.'

'I wonder if the folks who come would ask if that strange coloured hen would lay streaky brown eggs? I might say that it was a new sort of hen, which has been developed to lay streaky eggs to match streaky bacon.'

Esther laughed at the idea, Jackson continued following the same train of thought.

'It would be a winner in the hotels in the Lake District; over there they're daft enough to believe anything you tell them.'

'Keep your mind on what we were talking about, you haven't answered my question.'

'I don't recall you asking me a question. What was it?'

MUCK AGAIN!

'Don't you think it's about time you gave up that awful habit of chewing tobacco, it's very bad for your health.'

'Is it? Well, just you tell me why old Abel Simpson is still sitting in the pub most nights drinking ale and smoking his head off and he'll be ninety-one come Christmas?'

'Trust you to know somebody who's naturally very healthy. We can't all be that lucky.'

'You don't make much sense Lass. If it's a matter of luck, good or bad, then I have as much chance of dying before I'm seventy as the next man.'

'That's what I'm saying, they say that you can shorten the odds if you stop smoking tobacco.'

'I don't smoke it. There's a world of difference between smoking it when you draw it into your lungs … and spitting it out over a cheeky hen.'

'You're impossible to talk to. I only want what's best for you.'

'That's nice to know, but I have one or two questions to ask you.'

'Right! Go ahead.'

'First … how will I know on the day that I'm lying on my deathbed if I've managed to live longer than I would have done if I hadn't smoked and chewed tobacco?'

'You won't.'

'That's a good answer.'

'Next, how will I know if I've lost a few months or years because of my bad habit?'

'You won't.'

'Another good answer. My next question is … will I know whether any of my other bad habits have contributed to my early death?'

'You're being deliberately awkward. It's well known that people get lung diseases if they smoke.'

'Well now Lass, my lungs have been bad since I was dusted from working in the pits, just like a lot of other chaps, but all of us can do most things. Likely you don't know about such things, but the body copes very well and learns to compensate for the things that go wrong. Just look at Jim Nolan's black and white collie, she chases sheep and fetches the cows home with only three legs. And how about our Hoppelty? She can outwit your mother any day of the week and she's lost half of one leg.'

'You're being deliberately awkward again. What advice did the doctors give you when they told you that you were dusted? Did they tell you how to live healthily.'

'No, I remember him saying that looking at the x-ray he would have said that most of us shouldn't be capable of walking home from the surgery, but the same folks were leading active lives. He wouldn't have the cheek to tell any of us what we could or couldn't do. We don't ask him about his bad habits so why would he ask us what we get up to?'

' Some folks we can't help however much we try!' said Esther exasperated by the turn of conversation.

'But you know Lass, animals can chew tobacco and they seem to live as long as their mates in spite of it.'

'What sort of tale are you about to tell me now? I've never seen any animals chewing tobacco!'

'It wasn't one of ours.'

'Whose then?'

'It was few years back when your mother's niece Edie and her husband Joe lived in one of them cottages at Santon Bridge.'

MUCK AGAIN!

'It was a long time ago, I don't remember when they lived there, but I've heard Mam talk about it. They didn't keep any animals, apart from a few hens and a couple of ferrets; I can't imagine any of them smoking a pipe or chewing a length of black twist.'
Esther laughed at the thought.
'Aye, you may well laugh, but Joe used to enjoy a smoke of an evening after work. He would settle down in the wintertime in front of the fire, read his paper, then get out his tobacco from the dry cupboard at the side of the chimney, and light up.'
Esther watched the white streaky hen circling warily near them looking for titbits … and she wondered idly in which direction her father's conversation was going. Jackson took a piece of black twist from his pocket and sliced it with his usual care then placed it on his tongue.
'Come on Dad, if you have any idea of what you're going to say then get on with it. I have a strong feeling that you're making it up as you go along.'
'Well now Lass, when you've heard me out you can check the truth of the matter with Joe himself.'
'Huh! He'll only agree with you, men tend to stick together!'
'You can ask Edie if you like.'
'Don't worry I will.'
'Like I was saying, Joe enjoyed his smoke. Well it seemed to him that every time he went to the cupboard for his packet of tobacco it seemed to be going down much quicker than it should have been. It was costing him a fortune to keep his pipe filled. It was a real puzzle. Then he started to think that maybe young Harry was helping himself. When he mentioned it to Edie, she laughed and

reminded him that Harry was only nine and was unlikely to have started to smoke a pipe behind their backs'

'Could it have been Edie?' asked Esther mischievously.

'Don't be so daft, women gave up smoking pipes years ago.'

'I never knew that women ever did smoke pipes!'

'There you are, telling me how to live and die properly and you've never heard of women smoking! It was very common at one time. I used to see lots of women in Whitehaven sitting on their doorsteps happily lighting up their pipes.'

'I don't believe it!'

'Just you get yourself along to the library and ask for a history of Whitehaven, it'll tell you in there. It wasn't only in West Cumberland, it was a common habit in all industrial towns in the north. Women worked very hard in rough jobs just like their men did, so they copied what the chaps did. And why not? Nowadays you talk about equality, but it already existed in the mining towns where everybody worked like slaves with few pleasures except drinking and smoking. Women soon got a bad name if they went into the pubs, but nobody minded them enjoying a smoke. There weren't the fancy expensive cigarettes that women smoke in public places these days.'

'You could sell snow to Eskimos!'

'Anyhow, to get on with my true story, Joe was convinced that somehow his tobacco was disappearing from the cupboard even though Edie said it was impossible and that he was just lighting up a bit more than usual. Then one night when Edie had walked over to visit us, Joe fell asleep in front of the fire. Suddenly he woke up, something had disturbed him. He sat as quietly as he could thinking that an intruder was hanging about near the back door. Soon he became aware of a scratching in the tobacco cupboard. He got up silently from his chair and quickly opened the cupboard door just in time to see a huge rat disappear into a hole in the chimney. There was a trail of tobacco into the hole.'

'How awful! I'd be terrified of it.'

'What for? It was more terrified of Joe. He said he'd never noticed the hole in the back of the cupboard. It's surprising what a tiny hole a big fat rat can get through. He knew it must have been stealing for a good few weeks because he'd been missing his tobacco for a month or two. Wouldn't you reckon that the rat had formed a habit that it couldn't break?'

'I suppose it had.'

'You see Esther, most folks burn tobacco, but me and the rat prefer it dry. It's less bother than looking for a box of matches every five minutes, then struggling to light a pipe in wild and draughty places. It can lead to all sorts of accidents, many's the man or woman who's set the bed alight because they've fallen asleep while they've been smoking.'

'Did Joe catch the rat?'

'I never bothered to ask him, he was an expert on catching and trapping so I supposed he killed it. I'm sure he had no intention of sharing his tobacco with a bloody rat.'

'Fancy having a rat in your kitchen cupboard! That's awful!'

'Aye, it's bad enough if it eats you out of house and home … but to steal your tobacco! Now that's criminal!'

'Joe's always kept ferrets so he might have locked one in the cupboard to catch the rat.'

'I doubt that he'd do that, it's too messy. I don't think Edie would be too happy with that sort of slaughter. He probably put a trap in the cupboard ... or maybe he filled in the hole.'

'But if he did that the rat would be trapped in the wall.'

'Hardly likely, rats are very clever, they're like rabbits. they have the sense to dig escape tunnels even if they come out into the kitchen or a bedroom. Come to think of it he once told me that he'd seen one come out of the back of the fireplace when fallen asleep in the chair after coming home a bit late from the pub. He'd wakened to see a big rat eating the crumbs that had been dropped on the mat.'

'I'm sorry for anybody living in those cottages Dad, I wonder if they've seen any rats.'

'Nowadays folks are much more particular about things. The folks who live in these country spots say they love the countryside, but they pick and choose which animals they let into their homes.'

'How can you criticise them when you don't like rats ... you've always got plenty of traps set?'

'They eat my profits, that's a different thing, but at the same time you've got to admit that they're clever little things. It's time we went for dinner, I'm starved.'

Father and daughter made their way to the farm kitchen for their midday meal.

'The dinner smells good Edith,' said Jackson as he walked into the kitchen drying his hands as he went 'I'm hungry.'

'Me too,' said Esther.

MUCK AGAIN!

MUCK AGAIN!

'I can't see that either of you can be that hungry, you've leaned over the paddock gate for most of the morning while Bill's having to work as far from home as he can get.'

'We have been talking philosophy.'

Edith was surprised.

'What sort of philosophy was that Jackson?

'It was Esther really, not me. She was explaining to me that my life was going to be shortened because I chew black twist!'

'Quite right1 I'm glad you took some notice, but I wouldn't call it philosophy, I would call it common sense.'

'And he was telling me an unlikely tale about a rat which ate our Joe's tobacco.'

'That's true enough, but it's a sorry state of affairs when Edie could only get him to kill the rats when they decide to raid his store of tobacco. She'd been complaining for weeks about the rats, but he was too busy killing other folk's' vermin to find time to sort his own out.'

'Some women are never satisfied. A chap has to put his work first. It's like a painter and decorator who has a shabby house because he can't find time to paint it because the customer's house must come first.'

'Like a certain farmer who put the milk cans on the stand this morning and forgot to fill my jug.'

'Ah! So that's the reason for the marked lack of understanding! I thought you might be concerned about my early death.'

'It's more likely be in front of a firing squad of your relatives if you give us any more cheek!'

11.

PRIDE

Jackson felt very pleased with himself, he'd had a good morning, the ploughing had gone well and the weather had been kind. He washed his hands and walked towards the kitchen. Funny, that Edith hadn't called out to him as she usually did. Maybe she hadn't heard him come in.

He entered the kitchen and to his amazement was face to face with his sister-in-law. She was smiling broadly. She's maybe come to tell us she's marrying the vicar he thought to himself as he struggled to regain his composure. It was the first time May had ever visited them without prior warning. In addition, the warm smile was something he couldn't recall seeing before. This must be a momentous day – for some reason. He was about to greet her as he usually did, but he didn't get word out, May was already speaking to him.

'How nice to see you Jackson.'

Jackson wasn't sure whether things were getting worse or better. When she was openly antagonistic he knew where he stood, but this new May had thrown him completely. He had a strong desire to ask Edith to introduce him to this unknown woman.

'What brings you this far May? Judging by your face it must be good news. Are you going to marry again?' May's face momentarily looked as though the unaccustomed smile was about to crumble to be replaced

116

by its habitual disdain. However, she managed to maintain the beaming smile.

'Well. I felt that congratulations are the order of the day. So I've come along to say how nice it was to read about the triplets in one of the national papers. I didn't know that triplets in the animal world was a rare thing.'

Jackson smiled to himself, so this was the reason for the sudden warmth! The snobby old bugger!

'Aye, the story was a one day wonder.'

'Yes May, it was very exciting when the photographers descended on us,' said Edith as she dished up the pie.

'The best pictures were in the Farmers Weekly, did you happen to see them?'

'No Jackson, I never buy a trade paper. I don't usually buy the Daily Mirror but as so many people mentioned your success I felt I should purchase one.'

'Did many folks mention it in Egremont?'

'Yes Edith, I was surprised that so many people knew that I was related to you.'

'I bet it was the first time that she acknowledged it,' he muttered under his breath.

'What did you say Jackson, I didn't hear you clearly?'

'Nothing important, I only wondered if it was the first time anybody has mentioned our farm to you.'

May paused to reflect.

'I think you're right, farming matters aren't usually discussed in the shops ... apart from Wilson's, the butcher. He's always talking about freshly slaughtered meat. I do my best to avoid going there. I prefer the delicatessen shop further along.'

'What do they sell there then May?'

MUCK AGAIN!

'I thought everybody knew that Jackson. They sell cold meats, patés and specially prepared meat dishes They are a trifle dearer than the raw meat you can buy in the butcher's but their foods look so good on the table.'

'I'm glad you remember to treat yourself to these things now and again May, it'll do you the world of good.'

'I do, and the gentleman in the delicatessen speaks so nicely. I enjoy going there.'

'What's wrong with the way Lawrence Wilson talks? I can't say I've ever heard him swear and that's unusual for a butcher. Once they get among the blood and slaughtering, they tend to get a bit rough, but he's never struck me as being like that. Another thing, those fancy meats are only the normal meat camouflaged with a high price stuck on.'

'The Wilson's are from Egremont Jackson, he can't speak any other way. But the gentleman in the delicatessen is from the south and speaks so well, and a lot of preparation goes into the sort of meat dishes he sells. Most of them have French names, like the patés.'

As Jackson was about to open his mouth Edith quickly interrupted.

'After you've eaten you might like to have a look at the triplets May they're very beautiful.'

'Where are they housed?'

'At the far end of the byre, you'll see their pen after you pass that roan heifer that's tied up waiting for the vet to come with the A.I. equipment. He should be here in another hour or so. If he doesn't get a move on she'll have lost interest in things. I've always maintained that a good bull ..' Edith cut in sharply as she noticed May's face telling its own story.

'I think you'll like this apple crumble, just pass your plate over. The cream is especially fresh today.'

She glared in her husband's direction, but was met by a pair of mischievous twinkling eyes. She knew she mustn't leave the kitchen for a minute or else Jackson would set about shocking May. He had never understood her more refined outlook on life. She had lived in the south of England for a few years and experienced a different and gentler way of life.

'There's really no reason to see the calves I had a good look at them in the paper. And I noticed your dogs lying dozing outside that door with a big hole in the bottom. They don't seem to have the sense to lie down on a clean grassy bit, and if they jump up they might mark this new cream skirt or tear my finest nylon stockings.'

'Edith has a pair of wellies and a coarse apron you can put on to protect your clothes. I'm sure the calves would like to see you even though they've already had a crowd of press photographers and reporters and such like to admire them.'

'May is welcome to see them but I'm sure she would prefer to remain here, I don't often get the chance to talk to her these days.'

'Of course, but I'm so pleased about the publicity, like I said before, I understand from what I read in the papers that triplets are very rare. You must have done something right Jackson.'

'I had nowt to do with it. Congratulate the A.I. vet when he comes this afternoon. I'm not sure whether he made a mistake or not, but it's worked out well for us. I'll have to ask him to do the same again with that heifer that's wanting to be let out to join the rest of her mates. Modern methods can sometimes pay off May.'

'Yes I've always encouraged you to be progressive, and Edith has, at last, thrown her old-fashioned clogs away. Maybe you'll read the farming press more closely and introduce even more new ideas onto the farm.'

'The papers never noticed that we have two more sets of triplets May.'

'Goodness me! Why don't you send for them to come back and take more photographs? Success is so important it can lead the way for others who have less good management to learn and follow on.'

Edith knew exactly where her husband was leading the conversation and did her best to divert its direction.

'I'm sure that May isn't interested in the minor events of the farm. Shouldn't you be getting back to your work Jackson?'

'No Edith I want to hear about your other successes, I'm sure the people of Egremont would like to hear more about it.'

'Right May, I'll give you a bit more to relate,' he said meeting Edith's troubled gaze with innocent eyes.

'Yes May, triplets have been the order of the day for quite a few weeks on this farm. The first set was born to that young sow. She set the trend.'

'How many little pigs do they usually have Edith?'

'It depends, a young sow can't be expected to produce a big litter on her first farrowing.'

Aunt May nodded a bit uneasily.

'Then which animal had the next set of triplets?'

'Here's your cup of tea May, and do take a piece of chocolate cake, I know how much you like it. Never mind about the stock it's of little interest to anyone else except us.'

'No Edith, don't fuss when Jackson is explaining the new breeding patterns he has developed on the farm. National acclaim is a worthy achievement. Go ahead Jackson, tell me about the third set of triplets.'

'It was Hoppelty.'

'Surely you're not talking about that ancient hen that hobbles about the yard. The one with a quick temper if you inadvertently walk between her and her brood?'

'Aye that's the one. I didn't know that you'd noticed her.'

'She's vicious, I've always been a bit wary of the geese when I come here in the spring, but that little hen can be every bit as threatening as that horrible steg. But she always has a huge brood of chicks not just three. What sort of yarn are you spinning me Jackson?'

Her earrings spun as her annoyance grew.

'Like you May, we were disappointed with the pigs and the chicks,' said Edith 'and it seemed a bit unfair that one sort of animal was to be applauded while the other two were blamed for something they couldn't help.'

'You talk a load of rubbish at times Edith,' retorted Jackson, 'good farming produces good results and somewhere along the line we've made a mistake ... but they were all triplets, you can't deny that.'

'You always manage to twist events to suit yourself Jackson but there's no denying your success with the calves.'

A sound of a motor car driving into the yard interrupted the conversation.

MUCK AGAIN!

'Here's the vet, I'll ask him if he has the syringe he brought last year with a dose of triplets in! You never know your luck!'

Jackson rose and went out to greet the vet.

May shook her head in exasperation.

'Edith, I've gone to the trouble of making my way out here today to congratulate Jackson while all he can think of is that he has three piglets and three chicks as well as three calves. I admit these are disasters but if I were a farmer I wouldn't be so quick to present my disasters as being on a level with such a resounding success.

'Don't worry about him being able to accept success. I've heard plenty of tales about him boasting in the Grey Mare about his skill in breeding stock.'

'I wonder if he's so quick to tell them about the pigs and chicks.'

Edith laughed.

'I think not, I don't think anybody has been curious about them, the whole farming community is more interested in the triplets. It seems it's made farming history. But it was nothing that Jackson did.'

'No Edith, but I'm sure he will take all the credit if he can – at least in the pub. But he doesn't have an audience here, so he can make out it's an everyday thing. I'll never understand him Edith. However, that's enough about the farm, how is Esther getting on with her walking in the Lakes?'

'Very well, but she comes home worn out often with sore feet, but she says she loves it. It gives her the opportunity

MUCK AGAIN!

to meet different people, there are very few farmers who go walking.'

'You should encourage her Edith, she really shouldn't mix with farmers, it's not the sort of life for an intelligent young woman of taste.'

Edith could feel her temper rising as her sister spoke, but it was no use saying anything because May rarely listened to anybody else's point of view, she always felt she knew best.

'How about you May? Are you seeing John, if you don't mind me asking.'

'He writes to me. The letters are all very correct and proper. He would like me to meet him in Blackpool shortly, I believe there's to be a concert of classical and devotional music.'

'Do you think you will go?'

'Perhaps, he is sending me a copy of the programme ... '
At this point Jackson came back into the kitchen and sat down at the table.

'Another cup of tea Edith if the pot's still hot.'

He turned to May, what programme is that May? Are you going to a concert or show in Egremont?'

'Egremont! Of course not! Parochial entertainment is not for me I've been accustomed to attending proper theatres, not a village hall type of presentation.'

Jackson wondered what parochial meant but decided not to ask.

'The concerts that I've been to in the Parish Hall have been very enjoyable May, I'm sure you would see some of your friends if you went to a show. I'll let you know when I'm going next, you might like to come.'

'Thank you Edith, but don't go to any trouble, the truth is that once you have been to the best that a big city can offer then amateur performances are very much a let–down.'

'I've never been to a show like that, the Grey Mare offers good entertainment most week-ends ... and all for the price of a pint '

'Huh! You don't get beautiful music and the best actors in a pub Jackson. But I don't suppose you'd appreciate anything better since you've never experienced it. Many of the best things in life are acquired tastes, like good wine and serious music.'

'In that case May, what is the programme I heard you telling Edith about as I came in?'

May blushed and answered coyly.

'I was explaining to Edith that John had sent me a programme for concert of classical and devotional music.'

'Who's John?'

'Oh Jackson, you can't have forgotten the nice vicar that came to tea with May when I went as chaperone, you said yourself that in the neighbours might talk.'

Jackson's interest was immediate, he had forgotten all about the possibility of a romance, but things were obviously warming up a bit. The thought of May having romantic inclinations had seemed only remote a few months ago. He must certainly keep this new form of entertainment on the boil.

'You must go May, I imagine his intentions are honourable, and, as almost your next of kin I'm prepared to cast an eye over him. Just bring him here, I seem to remember inviting him when he came up here before but you seemed to think that he would have no interest in farming. But remember May that a lot of Bible stories are all about farming. I can tell the sheep from the goats May and I can find lost sheep as well as the next man, so if John needs a bit of hands on experience this is the place to come.'

'I'm sure John is very well trained in theology and can adequately answer questions about biblical stories without any help from an untrained person,' said May archly.

'Don't take any notice of what Jackson says, it's his way of saying that we will welcome him here.'

'Don't put words into my mouth Edith, preaching about saving souls is one thing but explaining the habits of flocks and herds is something that you've got to be brought up with. I could tell him some good tales about sheep and goats that would keep the youngsters who sit in the back pews wide awake.'

'Don't be silly Jackson,' snapped Aunt May, ' ... how can such a devout man stand up in the pulpit and tell a tale that is of doubtful origin? It's not like sitting in the bar in the Grey Mare!'

'No he can't,' agreed Edith.

'But if I remember rightly, from our Scripture lessons in Bookwell School, we were told that Jesus taught the ignorant people by telling them stories. I used to enjoy the Bible stories ... at least, when they were about animals or fishing. But the magic, healing bits, were beyond me, but I suppose it's hard for simple folks like us to believe that the sick were made completely better and could walk away on legs had never held them up for years.'

'I should think John will be able to explain it all to you,' said Edith hoping he would stop finding fault with May's suitor, to her it would be lovely if a marriage took place. The way Jackson was talking she might never get to know her prospective brother-in-law.

'Yes Edith, he's used to explaining the Faith to primitive tribes.'

'Well then, talking to me will bring back a lot of memories for him ... provided they're happy ones! If the savages stayed savage then his efforts would have been wasted. What made him come back from darkest Africa May?'

'He was needed back in this country Jackson. He has a church in a small town called Formby near Southport. He has a lovely parish there, ... so he tells me, naturally I've never been there.'

She blushed coyly.

'Not yet May!' smiled Edith.

'Is that the place where George Formby was born?" asked Jackson innocently.

'I have no idea,' snapped May, ' ... but I'm sure that anyone who speaks as badly as he does would be unacceptable in such a respectable place. It's where the very wealthy people who make their money in Liverpool choose to live. John loves his work there.'

'If he can make me laugh like George Formby does then you can fetch him along any day. He would be a big hit in the Grey Mare on a Saturday night ... I wouldn't expect him to go there on a Sunday. I must say that I'm looking forward to meeting my new brother-in-law.'

'No, no, Jackson, you have misunderstood me. We are only friends, you are jumping to conclusions, you can't expect a man of the cloth to rush into a marriage. A vicar's wife has to be a very special person. He told me that she has to be able to cope with anyone who calls to ask for succour … '

'Now we're back to the triplets, they ask for their succour from half past three onwards … '

'Oh Jackson! You know fine well what succour means.'

'No I don't Edith, I'm closer to them ignorant savages than you might think. I'd be surprised if they understood him if he used words like them.'

'I can see Edith, that the day I choose to call here will have to carefully thought out.'

'Come on a Thursday when I'll be out at the auction.'

'Strange as it may sound Jackson I'd be bringing him to see you.'

'Well there's quite a good likeness in the Daily Mirror, show him that.'

'Don't be silly Jackson,' said Edith, 'he'll want to get to know his future in-laws.'

'The best thing to do May if you're worried about him meeting your family, is to get married first then if he doesn't like us it's too late to do anything about it.'

'That would be very dishonest Jackson, but you both seem to think marriage is on the cards, but he's only invited me to go to a concert with him in Blackpool. I don't think that's a proposal of marriage.'

'You should take care May,' said Jackson mischievously. 'Be sure that you book into a hotel a long way from his, because you never know who is spending a weekend in Blackpool. It would keep the gossips in Egremont going for a week or so.

May was alarmed.

'Don't worry May,' said Edith soothingly. 'I'm sure you will be discreet, perhaps Esther and I could come with you for the week-end then there'd be no possibility of gossip should we be seen.'

It was Jackson's turn to look alarmed. The prospect of having to spend a weekend doing the cooking and washing the milking tins filled him with panic. He'd have to scotch this idea before it took root.

'Come now Edith, nobody came with us when we were courting, do you want to smother the poor chap before he's gathered his thoughts together.'

'We wouldn't stay with them, we'd enjoy going to a show, neither of us understands classical music, so we wouldn't go with May, we'd book into another show.'

Jackson was beginning to feel desperate by now, he must think of something.

He'd better think quickly of some way of escaping from this, he could see that Edith was getting the bit between her teeth. The only ray of hope was May's face. She was looking doubtful.

'You know May you're at the point when you'll have to be very careful to make a good impression and I don't think fetching your family along will be a good idea. He might think that they're there to look him over and I'm sure you can accept him or reject him without having to consult your sister and niece.'

Edith could scarcely hold her tongue only too aware of what her wily husband was thinking.

'He will be sure to do the correct thing Jackson, but I think maybe you're right. A family deputation might frighten him off … possibly he hasn't romance or marriage in mind so it might look as if Edith and Esther are vetting him.'

Jackson smiled happily. Things were back on track.

'Yes May,' he said warmly, 'I know you have far too much common-sense, you know very well how to arrange your personal affairs.'

May smiled again, 'I think as far as this invitation is concerned it would be better to go alone, but I will take care to book into a respectable hotel. There's a list of hotels in a brochure I have at home. I'll choose one on the sea front where I can merge with a lot of people and don't have to catch a trolley bus to go back there.'

'Very sensible May.'

'Yes Jackson, as John is always saying, everything is up to the will of God. I must go now or I'll miss the bus back. There's no need to set me on the way Edith, it won't take me more than ten minutes or so. I came to congratulate you on the success of your breeding programme and I'll certainly cut the photographs out of the paper to show John. I'm sure he'll be impressed.'

Edith saw her sister to the farm gate then returned to the kitchen.

'You certainly knocked the thought of a weekend in Blackpool for Esther and me on the head! You're always very good at looking after your own interests Jackson. You nearly tangled yourself up in your own web when you mocked John's vocation then had to do a turn-about in case you had to both look after yourself and do my daily work for a couple of days. It would serve you right if we plan a short holiday in Blackpool for ourselves!'

'Go ahead, just give me a week or so of warning,' he said airily, knowing fine well that the two women weren't likely to be bothered to organise things now that this surprise opportunity had gone!'

12.

ANOTHER BIRTH

'Has Peggy foaled during the night Bill?' asked Jackson as he entered the byre. It was early, about half past six and it promised to be a fine day.

'No, not yet, I had a look in the field as soon as I came out but she's grazing as if she has nothing to do, are you anxious?'

'No not really she's had a few foals so I should think things will be fine. I'm just weighing up what to do this morning, she can't do any light carting work because she's too fat to get between the shafts, so I think I'll do a bit of grubbing with her this morning she's able to do a bit of chain work.'

'Don't you think it would be kinder if you gave her a day or two off seeing she's about to foal?'

'Kind? I am kind. The best thing for her is to exercise if she lies about the foal gets too big and she won't be fit enough to cope with the foaling. But you young fellas don't know anything about giving birth. It's the same with women, it's best if they can keep working until the last minute then they have a trouble-free delivery.'

'I'm glad you're not a doctor, you wouldn't keep many patients with that attitude,' laughed Bill.

'Well now, in years gone by it was well known that women working in the fields often gave birth as they were working and just got on with what they were doing afterwards.'

MUCK AGAIN!

'That just shows how poor people were when they had to continue with the work to make a living.'

'Now that's just where you're wrong. I was reading a magazine your mother had left lying on the breakfast table the other day, and it was telling about a Queen, of somewhere in Spain I think. Her husband was always travelling about escaping from his enemies and his wife was very tough. She had her baby then got back onto her horse and rode on. Now then, who was it? All I know is that one of her daughters married an English king. Come to think of it, I think she married Henry V111 but I can't exactly remember. Did he marry a Spanish princess?'

'I'm not sure, all I know is that he had six wives.'

'Poor chap!'

'Don't feel sorry for him, he beheaded one or two, ask Mam she might know.'

'I suppose it's a quick way of stopping a woman from talking!'

' Why are you telling me such an improbable tale?"

'I'm only pointing out that even the rich can be sensible about birth while modern folks have problems that are in the mind. Women are guilty of letting problems build up in their imagination, when, if they just let things go naturally they would have a better chance of a painless delivery.'

'I wonder if Mam would agree with you?' laughed Bill.

'You can be sure she wouldn't agree, women have the knack of turning simple, natural things into complicated events.'

'What complicated events are you two talking about?' asked Esther as she came into the byre yawning her head off.

MUCK AGAIN!

'Getting up in the morning,' snapped Jackson 'what time of day do you think this is? The cows have been waiting to be milked while you've been asleep. Surely it's a simple enough thing to get out of bed in the morning?'

'Has Peggy foaled yet?' she asked ignoring her father's remarks.

'No she hasn't,' said Bill, ' ... so Dad is going to work her hard today to encourage her to foal and to keep her fit right up until the last moment.'

'That's the reason for 'making natural things into complicated events, I suppose. Well, it'll serve you right if she drops her foal in the middle of a stitch of turnips.'

'Oh no, there's no chance Lass, few mares foal during the day and Peggy is too well-behaved to do that.'

Esther nodded, 'I'm sure you're right, you and Peggy have a sort of telepathy going between you. Except that Peggy has a very sensible and placid outlook on life while you manipulate folks to do what you want!'

'Don't be so cheeky, if the mare could talk she might be more of a problem than me, after all she's a female of the species and they're always complicated.'

'I suppose a stallion would do as he was asked? The ones that call here to serve the mares are always dangerous and difficult to manage.'

'That's because they have such a lot of work to do in a short space of time and they have to walk miles to do it. I don't ask my mares to walk from Scotland to the Lancashire border and back. If I did, you'd soon be saying that I was cruel.'

'Trust you to twist things to suit yourself. Come on let's get on with things the weather's too good to waste the day talking a load of rubbish.'

MUCK AGAIN!

'Thought I saw you bringing Peggy home with gear on her back Jackson.'

'Yes you did.'

'Isn't her foal overdue?'

'Yes that's why I'm trying to help her. A bit of exercise is a good thing as you told me when you were expecting our babies.'

'Not to go harrowing or whatever you've asked that poor mare to do this morning.'

'Can't a chap get on with his work without the whole family finding fault? This is a farm, a place where horses have to work. Now if we ran a zoo or a maternity clinic things might be different, but we have to earn a living. Besides, she's not working this afternoon, I've put her on half a day. I hope that pleases you all.'

'Yes Dad, but I think you would have gone out again if we hadn't said something. I wouldn't have liked her to drop dead because the work was too hard.'

'Do animals ever drop dead because they've been overworked Dad? If anybody knows about such a thing it's likely to be you.'

'You'd think I was cruel to the animals, but not at all Lass, all animals need to work or they will lose their strength and fitness. But I do remember an animal dying of a heart attack.'

'Was it old-age it suffered from?' asked Bill suddenly interested.

'No, it happened when I was staying over in the Lakes.'

'It seems to me that the strangest of things always happened when you were over there in your young days.'

'Yes Esther, but I've told you before that they're not famous for their common-sense up them valleys.'

MUCK AGAIN!

'Just get on with your tale Dad and let us judge whether they're daft or not.'

'It was like this, one fine morning two of Jimmy's friends Jack and George called on their motor bikes to see if we would like to go up to a small farm at Dale Head where Jack's Uncle Frank lived. We were only too pleased to go. I rode pillion behind Jack while Jimmy rode with George. It was a lovely run up a very long valley. Dale Head was certainly the best name for such a remote spot. It was away up at the top of Wrynose Bottom, you turn left instead of carrying on up Hard Knott Pass.'

'That's the steepest Pass in the Lakes isn't it Dad?'

'Aye, it is that Lass. Well, we arrived at the farm and I was introduced to Jack's uncle. But the old chap was in a right way with himself. He said he was pleased to see us on our motor bikes because he had been putting a fat sow into the trailer when she must have sensed that things weren't going her way and bolted up the fellside. He was just about to start off after her when us lads appeared.'

He turned to Edith who was listening intently wondering if this story was true or not.

'Fetch another pot of tea Mother, it's thirsty work talking so much.'

'I expect you're used to lubricating your throat with a pint of ale when you're entertaining in the Grey Mare Dad.'

'If I'm the one doing the entertaining then I need to be helped along with a drink or two, so I expect some sort of support at home as well.'

As soon as Edith filled everybody's mugs Jackson settled comfortably to continue his tale.

MUCK AGAIN!

'Of course we said we'd be only too pleased to go up and fetch the sow back down. We looked up and could see her away up a grassy slope that wound its way up and over an outcrop of craggy rocks. She kept disappearing behind small clusters of rocks then reappearing a bit higher. 'Good God! It's awful steep up there' said Jack, but the bikes will manage fine.'

So off we went, but it wasn't long before us two pillion riders had to get down and walk. I must say I was glad to get off the bike, it was terrifying swinging and bumping about on the sheer slope. You know, the fells look easy from the bottom, but racing on a motor bike is another story. It didn't seem to bother the two lads whose bikes just screamed and roared as they zigzagged across the fellside. I think Jimmy and me were making as much progress on foot as they were on the bikes.'

'Poor animal, it must have been terrified,' said Edith sympathetically.

'You're right Mam, men have no idea how to deal with a frightened animal. The whole thing was a daft idea!'

'Do you want to hear my true story or not?'

'We do, go on Dad,'

'Like I was saying we were soon right up beside them, because they'd stopped and switched off their engines. They pointed across the fell and there was the sow making her way along the edge of a ridge, and below that was a sheer drop. So we decided to stand and wait because she might have the sense to turn round once she could see that there was another drop at the end. And, believe it or not, just as we were standing there willing her to stop and come back, she suddenly shivered all over and dropped like a stone! We knew instinctively that she was dead.'

'How terrible, you daft things had killed her!'

'No Edith we hadn't, if she hadn't have bolted she'd have been as right as rain.'

'Well,' said Esther, 'the only good thing is that she wasn't slaughtered in a noisy abattoir, but died up on those lovely fells'

'Good God Esther! We're in the business of fattening and slaughtering for the table, not undertakers!'

'What happened next? Serve you right if you had to carry her down on a motor bike!' said Esther hotly.

'As a matter of fact she was so heavy we had to pull and roll her back down to the farm. Uncle Frank wasn't too pleased but we'd only done what he asked.'

'Did he manage to butch the pig Dad?' asked Bill.

'I don't really know, but we went back a week or so later to help to saw up some fallen trees and Aunt Jane made us such a lovely tea. The rolled bacon was the best I've ever tasted!'

*　　　　　　　*　　　　　**　　*

'I'm not surprised that you're very quiet tonight.' Said Alan Steel as he walked up to the bar in the Grey Mare. Jackson looked up from his game of cards.

'I'm concentrating, it's about time I beat these three. They win so often that they're getting ideas above themselves. Anyway why shouldn't I be quiet, you seem to argue with everything I say when I do express an opinion?'

MUCK AGAIN!

Jackson knew that something was lurking in the back of Alan's mind, but he hadn't any notion of what it might be.

'Well, it's like this Jackson. For the last couple of weeks we've been invaded by photographers and newspaper reporters wanting to know about your triplet calves. But you've nothing to say about the latest birth on your farm!'

'What are you talking about?' asked a puzzled Tom Graham.

'It's obvious Tom. Peggy was overdue and she was such a size that she couldn't get between the shafts of her cart, so I was sure that Jackson was about to make history again with triplet foals! But there she was this morning with only one little filly foal staggering about.'

The listening drinkers laughed and waited for Jackson's reply.'

'Now then Alan, much as the whole country has been impressed by my skills as a breeder of first class shorthorns, and quite rightly so. With all the best will in the world, I can't work bloody miracles! At least, not twice in the same month!'

13.

HUNTING

'I wondered when you were going to hunt that old notice out Dad! It's been two years since Peggy had a foal, so I thought maybe you'd lost it.'

'No, I had always intended Peggy to have one or two more foals, she's a pedigree Clydesdale you know.'

'Oh I know, none of us are ever allowed to forget that we have a pedigree horse on the farm. Let's see the notice, it probably wants a touch of paint on it.'

Jackson held the notice up. It read.

BEWARE OF THE MARE AND FOAL

Esther laughed as she always did when she saw the notice.

'It's all very well you laughing, but it you'd be laughing on the other side of your face if somebody was chased as they walked along that public footpath through the field.'

'Yes Dad, we all know how dangerous Peggy can be for the first week after she's foaled. She won't even let us near her precious foal, let alone a walker often with a dog.'

'You know fine well that warning notices have to be put on gates where an animal is a danger to the public. Think of the heavy fine we'd have to pay if somebody was frightened or hurt by a galloping mare intent on chasing them back from where they came. It's only for a week or so then she settles down. She has to, because I need her to work at this time of the year. Like I keep telling you all, this is a working farm where animals have to earn their keep, not a public zoo.'

MUCK AGAIN!

'I've always wondered why you let her foal in that field when we could avoid the problem by putting her in the big field across the road.'

'Because she doesn't want to, s he has a favourite spot well away from the road where she likes to foal.'

'I thought you were in charge on this farm, not the animals! Besides, how do you know where she likes to foal?'

'Anybody who knows anything about horses knows when they're uneasy. I've tried a few times to get her to foal in the big field across the road, but she was restless and kept trying to dash back to the Paddock every time I opened the gate. It was as clear as if she was talking the Queen's English. At least, it was clear to me, but you young folks don't observe the animals closely enough. Another thing about it is that mares are often temperamental when they foal and Peggy is never like that normally. She's a great mare to have, so I think it's only fair that I let her have her way at this time even though I'm in charge of things for the rest of the year.'

'I didn't think you could look at things in that light Dad, I know there's a bond between you and Peggy because she lets you walk up to her and touch her foal long before she'll tolerate any of us going anywhere near it.'

'Maybe, but I'd have a problem if there was anything wrong with the foal, I don't think she'd let me handle it on the first day, but so far things have gone right.'

Esther brushed the dust off the notice.

'I think that will do, we don't need another at the other end of the path here in the yard. I'll get a bit of chalk and write a warning message on the gate in case we miss somebody walking through the yard. This fancy notice will look fine on the far gate, but you'll have to take it across the field Dad, I daren't!'

Bill walked over to join them and laughed when he saw the notice.

'We'll be the laughing stock of the district again! Every time you put that up folks ask me if we still have a vicious foal!'

'The general public has to be protected against its own ignorance. I take a very responsible attitude towards walkers. You've got to remember that farm animals and walkers don't mix. A cow will attack an intruder, especially when they have a calf. And have you never seen a herd of bullocks or heifers chasing after folks who stray into their field, especially if they have dog. Some folk have been killed just walking their dog through a herd of cows.'

'I've never heard of such a thing!' laughed Bill.

'If I had my way I'd have notices on all my field gates.' Esther laughed. 'Would that include corn fields and all arable land?'

'Yes it would, folks have no business walking across land that's planted, they do more damage than enough. I don't walk over their gardens and damage their lawns and flowerbeds! I think it's about time the public was educated about how to behave in the countryside.'

'A good idea Dad, but when I go walking on a Sunday we walk all over the mountains where the sheep are grazing, then we often walk right through the middle of the farmyard. Those farmers seem to put up with it without having Beware notices everywhere.'

'Aye well, that's a different story, they rely on visitors to stay in their houses, they've got to be prepared to put up with a bit of inconvenience. Apart from that, they never see a soul all winter so that they're really pleased when a new face comes through the gate.'

'I suppose it's hard to be married to a hill farmer on some remote farm like the one you went to and killed the poor fat sow.'

'We never killed her,' said Jackson hotly, 'she killed herself.'

'You yourself is always saying that animals can't commit suicide, so it must have been your fault for chasing her up the fellside.'

'Why is it that women twist everything you say so that they can use it to win an argument?'

'You see what I mean? Imagine living in a spot like Dale Head with a cantankerous, argumentative husband or father and not seeing another soul for weeks! It doesn't bear thinking about,'

'I thought you women believed in falling in love!' laughed Bill as he walked by.

'Now then lad, you're on to something important there. It's easy to fall for a lad or at a dance when he's tidied himself up and put on his best manners for an hour or so. A daft Lass is likely to think that that's what she'll get, but often that's not the case. I've been warning you Esther about these fancy lads who work at Sellafield, just take care and never judge by appearances.'

'Don't worry, I'll invite anybody I take a fancy to for a long walk up Wrynose bottom then up to Dale Head to see if the silence and loneliness frightens them.'

'Have you finish Bill? It's time we went for our breakfast.'

MUCK AGAIN!

They sat at the breakfast table thankfully eyeing the bacon and eggs. Jackson picked up the paper which had just been delivered and started to read it.

'Just listen to this Bill, there's a group for protesters here who want to ban hunting, I've never heard of such rubbish!'

'It's long overdue if you ask me,' said Esther as she tackled her breakfast. ' Why can't they leave the wild animals alone, there's enough slaughtering goes on with domestic animals so let the others live.'

Jackson looked as though he was about to burst a blood vessel.

'So, you would let the foxes kill our poultry?'

'There must be kinder ways of getting rid of animals Dad, it only takes a bit of imagination.'

'Take no notice of Esther, she doesn't understand what she's saying. She only wants to aggravate you.'

'Esther is right, there are other ways of getting rid of vermin, but the folks who want to stop hunting have no understanding of the way the countryman's mind works. It's really just a question of psychology.'

Esther lowered her knife and fork in astonishment at this new, thinking, father she had sitting opposite her.'

'Go on! Explain a bit more.'

'I'm sure I've explained this before, but you never listen. It's like this, over the centuries country folks led very uninteresting lives. The entertainments were mostly in the cities, so folks made their own fun. So, what they did was to tart up the nasty jobs. Now the wealthy, especially in the south of the country dressed up in smart red coats, led out their best hunters and galloped about across the likely hiding spots for foxes. I'm sure most of them weren't a scrap interested in killing the foxes. The fun was in the chase, just like courting, the catching can be a bit of a disappointment.'

Esther glanced at her mother whose eyebrows lifted only slightly.

'Women especially, who ride with the hounds have a different quarry altogether in mind.'

Esther chuckled. 'Trust you to see things differently!'

'I see things as they are Lass. Fox hunting in the south is a spectacle. The fox often outwits the dogs and riders because it's cleverer than most of them.'

Edith shook her head in exasperation.

'What about hunting up here? We don't ride to hounds around here.'

'No, because the terrain isn't suited to those prancing hunters, they'd be likely to break a leg trying to cross the rocks. It's the followers on foot who support our sort of hunt, but it's a young fit man's sport, it wouldn't suit their Lordships in the south. There's too much footwork involved for them.'

'Only the Master of the Hunt dresses up in this area, the rest of them just need strong boots and plenty of energy.'

'Yes I've noticed that Mam, but a lot of folks follow in their cars to watch the dogs racing across the fells. I can understand them, the chase is very exciting as the fox streaks across the fellside and weaves in and out behind the rocks and up the side of the becks, but I wouldn't like to see a kill.'

'No, you're like a lot more, you like the killing and slaughtering to be done out of sight, but in farming, slaughter is all part of making our living.'

MUCK AGAIN!

'Yes, it's all very sad, the groups who want to ban fox hunting because it's cruel, never think of banning slaughtering for food.'

Jackson was looking decidedly uneasy.

'Where on earth do you get such daft ideas from?'

He turned to Edith.

'I knew it was a mistake for her to join that Rambling Club. Anybody who wants to trail the length and breadth of the countryside as a pastime can't be able to think straight, if you ask me. The likes of us who have to walk miles every day as part of our day's work have a good excuse, but just to wander aimlessly shows a lack of common sense. Next Sunday you can do a bit of harrowing, that'll keep your feet busy.'

'You jump to conclusions Dad, I don't need to ask other people to give me opinions. Living among animals makes me attached to them, I hate to see them go to be butched. I don't think I should be ashamed of growing to love the stock ... and come to think of it some of them were here before I was, they have more reason to be here than I have!'

'Huh! I never knew you were so concerned about the fate of our fatstock. What concerns me more is who buys the meat.'

'What do you mean by that Jackson? I've never heard you talk about the shopper who buys our meat?'

'Well now Edith, if I ever get to thinking about the fat pigs or sheep or cattle we've bred for the table, my worst nightmare is if I take to imaging some daft woman, or even a chef burning or spoiling the dinner. It makes all

MUCK AGAIN!

our breeding and feeding a waste of time. The poor beast has died in vain!'

Esther laughed, 'I never thought of you imagining things like that!'

'Well I can't abide waste. But you know Esther, going back to hunting, you're like everybody else ... all you think about is fox hunting. But the best sorts of hunting are never mentioned.'

'What are they?'

'Rat and rabbiting, I've spent a good many hours enjoying hunting them damned pests and nobody waves a notice under my nose objecting to my hunting.'

'I suppose you're right, I don't have any second thoughts about rats being killed.'

'There you are, you're not really an animal lover. You only like the well-behaved cuddly ones. But talking about rabbiting, I remember Joe, Edie's husband went off on his bike to catch rabbits on a farm about ten miles away down the coast somewhere near Silecroft. The farmer was fed up with them eating his young crops and he had no idea about catching rabbits. So, like I was saying, Joe got the job and off he set early in the morning about half past six because it takes a good while to bike that far with nets and a box of ferrets on his back.'

'Is this true Mam?' asked a suspicious Esther.

'If your Dad says so I suppose it must be.'

'You can always ask Edie like you did when I told you about the rat that ate the tobacco. I don't mind if you never believe a word I say, but my tales bring good trade to the Grey Mare I never get any complaints from Jean, so you can always go outside and finish swilling the byre floor.'

MUCK AGAIN!

'No, I think I'd rather listen to your tales than swill the byre.'

'Like I said, Joe left home very early, but about ten o'clock when Edie was busy washing the clothes in the kitchen, she happened to look out of the window and was surprised to see something moving about in the bushes at the bottom of the garden. She was scared that it was a rat, she'd had enough of them when the one I was telling you about took up residence in her cupboard, so she was nervous about investigating the shaking bushes. But as she watched two little animals jumped out and started to play in the sunshine.'

'They were Joe's ferrets?'

'That's right, he was amazed when he reached his destination to find the ferret box empty, he'd never heard them get out of the box on his back, nor had he the least idea how far he'd gone before they'd escaped.'

'That's like the story of the two pigs that got out of the trailer when they were on their way to Haile!'

'Aye, Jane Mossop's saddleback gilts, they had a good home. But ferrets are different, they love to hunt so why did they jump ship?'

'You, Jackson, give animals motives for their behaviour, when they act by pure instinct.'

'Since when have you studied animal behaviour Edith? Animals soon have us weighed up, believe me. But you're right about instinct. Take homing pigeons, they can find their way home from foreign lands, so why can't pigs and ferrets do the same? The ones I know certainly could.'

'Did Edie put the ferrets back in the stable where Joe kept them?'

MUCK AGAIN!

'That was one of the strange things about Edie, she was as frightened of ferrets as she was of rats. She stayed in the house, not even going out to hang the clothes out until Joe got back home and picked them up. It's a wonder they didn't disappear down a drain looking for rats. Women can be really daft at times.'

'I don't like rats or ferrets either Dad.'

'Just have a close look at them next time they cross your path and work out how many times bigger you are than one of them, it must be hundreds. Next, imagine a rat as many times bigger than you! Then decide how lucky you are that it's the right way round for us.'

'I've never heard such reasoning before!' said Edith sharply. 'Don't you think it's time you got on with some work and let me get on with mine?'

'Aye, well I'll just take this Beware notice and nail it to the far gate before you ask me to add other vicious animals to the list like rats, rabbits and ferrets!'

'I could add the name of another inhabitant of this farm that visitors should be wary of!' said Edith tetchily as she began to clear the table.

14.

A RELATIVE COMES

'Where is cousin William? I expected to see him in the byre this morning to watch us doing the milking.'

'He was up very early and your father took him off to look round the farm.'

'Good he'll see what a small mixed farm is like, but Mam, can you tell me more about my Uncle Bill? Dad has always been cagey about him when I ask questions.'

Edith laughed and nodded.

'It's a strange story, but it's true. Your Dad's brother took himself off to join the army at the beginning of the first World War. A lot of daft young men did the same thing, there wasn't much work here and young men think that war is all adventure, and they were also told that it would soon be over. So off they went to cover themselves in glory. Your father thought of going, but I soon talked him out of that idea.'

Esther chuckled she could imagine her mother putting her foot down.

'But my own brother, who was also called Bill, went off leaving four small children, one only a tiny baby, and was killed on the Somme. I often wondered what his death gained for this country. And, as you know your cousins gained a stepfather who was a drunkard and spent all his money in the pubs in the town. Your poor Aunt Hettie lost one good husband and gained a very bad one ... and three more children.'

MUCK AGAIN!

'What a shame, but she wouldn't know how things would turn out, she likely thought she was doing her best for her children.'

'She did, but it's sad to say that when the new husband died of pneumonia, I think she breathed a sigh of relief.'

'But what can you tell me about this Uncle, Dad's brother?'

'Like I said he joined up and was shipped off to fight in France in the trenches. He sent his father one or two letters, as your father has told you, their mother died when they were small. He wrote as best he could, because the lads went to school only when their father remembered to send them. But he told how bad the conditions were. The mud sucked some of them under if they were unlucky enough to slip off the boards, which criss-crossed the battlefields. He thought Hell couldn't be much worse.'

'But he came home safely?'

'No, it wasn't as simple as that. A lot of the lads deserted and were shot, but he wasn't shot.'

'He was a deserter?'

'I don't blame any of them who made a dash for it. Dying like rats in a hole is no way to lay down your life for your country.'

'He must have got away because he lives in Chicago now.'

'He did, he slipped away from France with the Canadians. He knew that he could never return to England. So he went to Canada and then crossed into the States. I think it was very hard for him there because he tried to farm and farming in the Midwest isn't like farming on the West Coast of Cumberland. So I believe he works for a beef canning firm, I think he buys animals to butch, I'm sure your cousin William Junior will be able to fill in the gaps.'

'I've not had chance to say much to him he arrived so late last night. Fancy hiring a car at Liverpool! He must be quite wealthy to do that. How long is he staying?'

'I think only a day or two, he wants to meet the rest of your Dad's family.'

'I'm glad he came here first, that gets the worst over first!'

'Your father isn't as bad as all that, he can be very sociable when he tries, and after all it's his own family he won't be likely to treat this lad like he does your Aunt May.'

'But he's unlikely to be as snobby as Aunt May either. You know something Mam, he looks very like our Bill, he has the same curly black hair and stands about the same height. But the image was broken the minute he opened his mouth, he sounded like Roy Rogers!'

' I know, Jackson's brother's lad should sound like us!'

'I've got a huge beef pie in the oven and apple crumble with custard for dinner at twelve, I hope he likes it.'

'He should, I'm sure they eat ordinary food like us in the States. I believe they like a full plate.'

'That's easy, do you think I should bring my best embroidered tablecloth out and put a small vase of flowers in the middle? I want to give a good impression.'

'I wouldn't, he wants to see how we live. I'm sure his Dad will want to know all about it and when he describes the oilcloth on the table it'll bring back memories for him. You know Mam, it's terribly sad when an Englishman daren't come home to see his family. Would he be shot now after all these years?'

'I believe so. One day there may be an amnesty, so you never know if he'll come to see us sometime.'

Esther was excited when she heard footsteps crossing the yard shortly after twelve. The two men washed their hands in the back kitchen then came through to sit at the dinner table.

'What do you think of our farm then William?'

'It sure is small Esther, the ranches where I go to buy steers for slaughter are many miles across, we can't walk the farm like we've done this morning. Another thing that surprises me is the way it is truly mixed. You have a bit of everything, pigs, beef and dairy cattle and poultry of all kinds. In the Midwest farmers tend to specialise. There are many acres of wheat as well as the huge ranches.'

'I don't think I would like that, I like a lot of variety.'

'You certainly have that. You seem to have a variety of breeds that I never see. All the steers we buy are Hereford, which is an English breed.'

'We have very few of them up here,' said Jackson, 'they're a breed from the south of the country. Up here we prefer a mixture of dairy and beef cattle; the milk cheque is what keeps us going on a day to day basis.'

'I've seen lots of them on cowboy films. I wonder if there are any other breeds in America.'

William laughed.

'We sure have, but the filmmakers aren't interested in dairy cattle being herded at breakneck speed by the actors. However, milk shakes are very popular in our country, so we certainly have large herds of what you call milk cows. But my father and I buy the beef breeds because Chicago is still the centre of the beef industry.' Esther wondered if he knew about his father's war experiences.

'You must come over to see us,' he said as if he was reading their thoughts, 'as you know my father can't come over here but he'd like to see you all again.'

Esther glanced at her father and thought she saw the hint of a tear in his eyes.

'I doubt your uncle will ever do that William, it's too far and we can't leave the farm, but we often speak of him. Do your friends and neighbours know his story?'

'Of course, many people do. He belongs to an ex-servicemen's Club where there are quite a lot of deserters. Naturally they have regrets because they can never return to their native land, but life is much better than death and they support one another. They were all far too young to face the horrors of that awful war. Things were very bad for my father when he first crossed into the States from Canada. He had to leave Canada because it is English territory and if he had been identified he would have had to answer to British law. The land here was too difficult for him to cultivate, you have to understand the changes of weather here. So once he'd met my mother he decided to look for work, which he found near Chicago and he's never looked back since.' He addressed his next remark to Bill.

'You should think of coming over Bill, life is much easier and the money a lot better than anything you can make on a small farm like this one. I'll tell my father that he certainly made a good decision when he joined the Canadians and got out of that Hell-hole.'

MUCK AGAIN!

Edith looked uneasy and glanced in Bill's direction to see if he was interested.

'It's worth thinking about William, it must be easier to work for somebody else than to slog it out on a small farm barely making a living.'

'But nowadays,' said Esther who had seen her mother's anxiety, 'the new Nuclear Plant at Sellafield offers a much better living than farming does, so a lot of farmers' sons are getting good jobs there.'

'Aye, farmers and miners make good reliable workers down there.'

'Yes Uncle but you don't have the attractions of a big city like Chicago on your doorstep. We go to the best concerts and Shows and there are huge sports arenas. Life in America offers much more than a small town like Egremont.'

'This afternoon we're taking you to see your Uncle Fred, he has less stock than we have. He has a few cows for milk and thousands of sheep scattered on the fellside.'

'A fellside, what's that?'

'A mountain,' said Esther laughing. 'I don't suppose you have mountains near you! At least I haven't seen any near the cowboy trails on the films.'

'No Cousin Esther, the Rockies are a very long way from us, I reckon this little island would get lost in the Midwest and wouldn't reach to the Rockies. '

'I've read about the wagon trains going over there in the Geographical Magazine so from what you say it must have been a long journey.'

'It sure must have been Uncle Jackson, it took months of travel to get over to the eastern seaboard, but for those who made it the climate in Nevada and California is

156

warm and sunny and the soil is very fertile once it is irrigated. Some the films give a fair idea of how brave those early settlers were.'

'Many had gone to America to escape religious persecution, so to land on the eastern seaboard then to trek overland all those thousand of miles to the west in search of peace must have been a great act of Faith.'

'You certainly know about American history Aunt Edith.'

'I read a lot.'

'And she spends a good many hours in the Picture House as well,' interrupted Jackson.

William laughed, 'so do we, that's where we learn a lot of our history as well, it's better than what they tell us in school. But I'm here to meet my father's family and to look at some of the historical buildings in this country. We have no castles, my father says I have to take a photograph of Egremont Castle. I'll send a postcard of the Castle later today, I know it's only a ruin but I believe you were raised just beside the castle.'

'Yes, we were but tonight we'll go the Grey Mare and tomorrow we can go into a few pubs in Egremont that your father will remember.'

'I'm looking forward to that Uncle Jackson.'

Three days later as Edith and Esther were preparing the sheets for the wash the atmosphere in the farmhouse was lighter.

'I'm glad William junior enjoyed his stay with us. At least he seemed to have a good time.' 'In spite of your father's efforts to get him drunk!'

MUCK AGAIN!

'It wasn't a conscious effort on his part Mother. The locals in the pubs were so welcoming that he felt obliged to drink what was offered.'

'I don't think he had any problem. I fear that a liking for drink runs in the family!'

'Mother, you were worried to death in case Bill was tempted to go off to America, but I don't think he will. One day we may go for a short holiday, but I know that I wouldn't like to stray that far from here. I'd miss the fells and the lovely walks I go on.'

'That's right Pet, it doesn't matter where you fancy going but at the end of the day there's no place like home. I know your Dad isn't interested in going, it's much too far, and he's never been out of the County in his life. I know he's happy enough travelling with the Geographical Magazine. He travels all over the world from his armchair and I'm glad he's happy with that. We can't really afford to visit relatives so far away.'

'Another thing Mam, I had a strong feeling that he looked down on us because we don't live the sort of life they do over there. I know he's my relative on Dad's side but he often gave me the feeling that he was related to Aunt May!'

'You've found your way back here then!' greeted Bill Brown as soon as Jackson entered the Grey Mare.

'Where do you think I'd be then?'

'We thought you might have gone to America with your nephew. A very nice lad, but he hasn't learned to take the beer like you, but in time he'll develop his family tendencies.'

'Aye, you're right Bill,' agreed Frank Bates who was standing at the bar.

MUCK AGAIN!

'I think the lad had his work cut out trying to drink all the pints everybody bought him. And you are right Bill, you can't expect a young chap to cope with his drink like we can, it takes a good few years of dedicated practice to get it right. But he made a valiant attempt and did the family credit. Anyhow, I'd like to thank you all for being so pleasant to him, I think he had an experience he'll never forget. He's off to have a look round some castles down south before he takes the boat from Liverpool. They don't have anything of any great age in America.'

'Did he have a look at Egremont Castle?' asked Jean as she pushed Jackson's pint across the bar.'

'Yes he did, it's a shame that we have one of the few ruined castles in the area, but we all went down to have a look at Muncaster Castle. Later, Edith and Esther went in the car with him to Carlisle to have a look at the Castle and the Cathedral there. He enjoyed the day. Mind you I've never been into the city, the auction Mart is the only place I've see at Carlisle. I've no real curiosity about where we locked up the Scots.'

Jackson made his way to his favourite seat and prepared himself for any banter that might be aimed in his direction.

'Just think Jackson it might have been you returning to England to visit your relatives if you'd answered the call to join Kitchener. I reckon you missed out there, I liked the car, but you haven't got round to buying a tractor yet.'

'Aye, well I thought about joining Kitchener but I didn't reckon the uniform would suit me. If you're six foot tall an army uniform looks good, but my girth is as long as my inside leg, so I lost interest before the start. Another thing you have to remember is that a lot of chaps had a houseful of kids, so a year or two in France would give everybody a rest.'

'That's not very patriotic!'

'You bet it is Frank, why do you think the government is so keen on wars? The answer is pure and simple … it's poverty, we have too little food and too many people to eat it. That's been the case throughout history, it's always been a favourite way of culling the population. It might be cruel, but if they make it out to be a glorious sacrifice then even the young, daft ones rush to sign up to get themselves killed.'

'That's a stupid way of thinking Jackson.'

'You might think so Frank, but unfortunately it's the truth.'

'Which category did your Bill fall into?'

'The young and daft one. There was only the pits and farming here and the thought of travelling to foreign countries like France and Belgium wearing a uniform and enjoying free food sounded like adventure. Besides, the recruitment campaign in Whitehaven was well organised, just as it was throughout the land. Ignorant lads were swept up in the excitement of it all. They were going to thrash the Germans in a few months just to teach them a lesson. The uniforms would scarcely get dirty. The only thing was the Germans were running an equally efficient campaign and they had the advantage of fighting near their own homeland.'

'I think what Jackson says is the truth, but it's usually a woman who talks that sort of sense,' said Jean hotly.

MUCK AGAIN!

'We don't expect any contribution from behind the bar, women should just mind their own business and not offer opinions about things they know nothing about.'

'We know all about it Frank. The lads that died in the trenches were calling for their mothers, not their fathers or the recruitment officer.'

'We came here for a quiet drink, if we want a sermon we can go to church!'

'I reckon it's about time some of you went to church.'

'The vicar doesn't like us to come in here so watch what you say.'

'Church isn't for me either,' said Jackson, 'they like to talk about the glorious dead, whether they die in the war or not. I like to take one world at a time and I prefer the glory to be here when I can enjoy it.'

'Don't let your Edith hear you say that Jackson.'

'I say it many a time Jean, but she just says that I'll probably see the light one of these days. She reckons I'm a slow learner.'

'But to get back to our conversation, I wonder why your Bill hasn't come over to see you if his son was coming. Maybe he feels he's too good to mix with the likes of us.' Jackson had been waiting for this remark because rumours always spread when lads didn't come back from the war.

'Now then Frank, that's not an easy question to answer. I'm pretty good at answering for myself, but not much of a hand at answering for somebody else. That's the way to mislead folks. But I would say that before the war there was little work for us, and even less after the war. If more lads had been killed then finding jobs would have been easy, but them lads that could think things out wanted no more of the way this country had treated them so went to build new and better lives in the States. But, I'm only guessing. You can ask him yourself the day he comes back home.'

One or two sly smiles went round the bar. Jackson was quite capable of defending himself.

'Oh Frank, before I go over to my game of dominoes, maybe you could call at the house, Edith wants to hire your lorry to move some old furniture to the rubbish tip, we have a new three piece coming next week and she needs to clean the parlour before it arrives. Women are always changing things, that sofa was good enough for my mother and father so it should last us a bit longer.'

'They've been dead about twenty years Jackson!'

'I know Jean, but nobody ever sits in the parlour except at Christmas and on funeral days, but when William came she said she felt that it was too shabby ... so I reckon I won't be inviting my relations from America in a hurry, it's much too expensive!'

15.

VISION

'**I** have made an appointment for you for tomorrow morning at the surgery Jackson, so you can ask Tom to run you in to Egremont. If we want to go we have to walk, but I know you will never get there if you have to walk and I can't imagine you going on horseback these days.'

'What on earth made you decide that I need glasses? I haven't any use for a pair. When do I ever read a book?'

'Never, but you try to read the magazines you like and you get it all wrong. Only last week I heard you ask why the writer of an article advised you to keep a dairy and you said you'd done it for years then when I picked up the article it said you should keep a diary. Then that cheque you signed for the South Cumberland Farmers looked funny and when I had a closer look you'd signed it in the wrong place.'

'Did they send it back?'

'No, it wasn't that bad, but if you can't see well then things can be dangerous.'

'I don't drive, except the horses and both of them have very good eyesight, so I can't see the problem. As for the Farmers Weekly I'm better off without it. It only encourages wild spending that we can't afford. The cheques are of no importance either, they always find a way of getting money from you so I'm not bothered about that.'

MUCK AGAIN!

'You always have an answer for everything we suggest. I thought you might find reasons not to go so I made the appointment for you.'

'Why don't you go if you're so keen on having a pair of reading glasses in the house. If you get some then I can borrow yours if I need to read anything important.'

'My eyes don't work like yours, you could damage your eyesight if you use somebody else's. You also need to go to the Bank and you enjoy a pint in the 'Black Bull' it's a long time since you were in there.'

'Is it? You seem to keep close tabs on me!'

'I like to know what you're up to.'

'I can't get up to much when your nosey sister goes down the Main Street most mornings.'

'She doesn't go into the 'Black Bull!'

'Maybe not, but I have to walk in from the street and then walk out again to Tom's car ... and how much would you bet that she knows about it either then or later in the day?'

Edith ignored the question and continued reading the post. 'And another thing Edith, I might start seeing things I've not really seen properly for years and I might get some unpleasant surprises. Come to think of it, I haven't seen you too clearly for the past few years and I could get quite a shock when I come home, I might think I've got the wrong house. Worse still from your point of view I might cast an eye over some smart young woman I spot walking down the street.'

'She's welcome to you, you would only have work and worry to offer her, so I don't feel in any danger of losing you.'

MUCK AGAIN!

'The reasons for new glasses seem to have gone so I'll pass them by. In any case where would I keep a pair of specs? It's bad enough trying to keep track of my black twist and the few pence I carry around in my pocket without learning to cope with useless glasses at my age. And what's that letter you're reading?'

Jackson was always suspicious of letters, they usually heralded some sort of unwelcome change to his comfortable routine. Invitations were the worst, both Edith and Esther would be off at the drop of a hat. Weddings were very popular, as were holidays with relatives in the Lake District.

'It's not a family letter, but a programme of evening study at the Parish Hall in Egremont. Evening classes are very popular these days.'

Jackson scented danger, 'I think you're too old to go back to school Edith, the brain runs out of working cells by the time it gets to your age.'

Edith looked up in astonishment.

'I can think as well as I did when I was much younger, in fact some of the decisions I made when I was a twenty something don't bear close scrutiny.'

'I have a feeling that remark was aimed in my direction.'

'If the cap fits, wear it.'

'All this unpleasantness because I don't want to have my eyes tested.'

'Don't be silly, you need glasses. But my brain needs a bit of stimulation, there's not much inspiration on a farm.'

'It's William from America that's brought this on. You were happy enough until then. I think that visitors should be discouraged, it only unsettles you.'

MUCK AGAIN!

Edith ignored her husband and was eagerly scrutinising the programme of subjects available.

'Yes, quite a few of these would be suitable I think everybody should support the Church in its efforts to educate the older generation.'

'I thought its job was to get people into Heaven! I thought education was what the schools were there for!'

'There were some folks, like you, who rarely went to school, and the Church in its wisdom wants to provide an opportunity for intelligent people to improve their education as well as offering a social event.'

'It's the social bit I think is wrong for you.'

'How is that?'

'When you go to the pictures I know what time it finishes so I can expect you home in an hour or so later. But if you're sitting sewing or something like that and talking with the other women, you'll not notice the time, and I'll be sitting here at home worried to death about where you are.'

'What rubbish! I never bother myself when you are sitting drinking and cracking in some pub or other. When you go to the auction with Tom you could be in one of a dozen pubs in Whitehaven, I never know. You could be knocked down in the street and I wouldn't know, but I decided years ago that's your own decision, so I don't let it worry me.'

She looked down the list of evening courses.

'Ah! Here's the very thing for you – Accountancy. It's time you did the paper work.'

'That's why you want me to have a pair of glasses!'

'Sewing and knitting aren't for me, they wouldn't shake up my brain,' she observed.

MUCK AGAIN!

'How about a Cookery Course? We could do with a change from stews and pastry dishes! Do they offer any French cookery.'

'Cookery comes into the same category as the knitting and sewing. Ah! Here we are … Make-up lessons. It says you can soon look years younger if you just follow this Course. Yes, when I go to the Mothers' Union on Thursday I'll put my name down.'

Jackson was almost speechless.

'I thought you were going to improve the inside of your head, not muck about with what's past renovation! Is there nothing else on that list that you could make a success of?'

Edith perused the list, then shook her head.

'Only French and Italian for Beginners and Gymnastics Level 5'

'Take the Accountancy then at least you might learn where our money goes.'

'I don't need to go to Night Classes to know that most of it finds its way into the till in the Grey Mare!'

*   *   *

'Nice to see you in town Jackson, what brings you here before opening time?'

'Hello Albert! Edith says my eyesight's going so I'm getting my eyes tested.'

'A good idea, your eyes are too important to neglect.'

'I'll never wear the bloody things, I'll probably lose them as soon as I get them, but, as you know, women have to be pacified, it's much easier to agree and to go along with whatever they decide. If it was a matter of principle, now that would be a different matter. Anyhow the Black Bull will be opening its doors soon so Tom Graham and me will spend an hour or so keeping the barman happy.'

'Good idea, but talking about your Edith, isn't that her sister May over there looking in the jeweller's window.'

'Is it? I didn't notice her.'

Albert laughed, 'I think you do need glasses when you can't see your own sister-in-law.'

'It has little to do with my eyesight, it's just that I don't particularly want to meet her, she's a snob and never wants to acknowledge me! Although she might do today because I've polished my boots and haven't brought the horse and cart with a load of muck for somebody's garden!'

Albert chuckled.

'Well she did marry one of the Douglas's, so she probably feels that she's important.'

'Just a minute Albert! Did you say that she's looking in the window of the jeweller's shop?'

'Yes, she's still there and she's talking to that smart looking Ada Burns and pointing to some trays of rings or necklaces. Why are you interested?'

'Oh nothing, I can make her out now, she's moving off towards her house, so I don't have to think of something polite to say to her. Here's Tom coming now, so I'll be off, we want to go down to the Farmers' Supply to see if they've got owt new in the way of calf meal.'

Jackson mused to himself as he and Tom made their way to the bottom of the street.

'What are thinking about Jackson, has Albert said something to you?'

168

'Aye, he said he'd seen Edith's sister looking at rings in Bawden's window.'

'So? What's wrong with that? The shop is open to everybody.'

'I know that Tom, but May? She's been seeing a chap when she goes to Blackpool. It could be that he's popped the question. It's strange that Edith hasn't said anything.'

'What sort of chap is he? He must be a real gentleman to suit her!'

Jackson had no intention of informing the entire district that there was a possibility that he might have a vicar for a brother-in-law. He wouldn't be able to enter any pub without sniggers and even outright laughter coming his way. If the silly old thing was buying an engagement ring then things were looking serious. Out loud he said 'I know very little about him, I'm sure he's a gentleman, she's a very fussy woman … but I'll have to have a word with him.'

'Why?'

'She's so stuck up … and her last husband was nagged to death, I feel it's only the decent thing to warn him.'

'But Jackson, she's a smart looking woman. She dresses like a much younger woman and wears make-up, fashionable hats and plenty of jewellery, you have to expect chaps to look her over.'

'It just shows that folks judge by appearances, but it'll take a lot of money to keep her in the height of fashion. Besides she's been a widow for a few years now and has got into the way of having her own way, she'll take badly to doing as she's told. Like any old mare … she'll take a lot of retraining.'

Tom laughed as they walked into the Farmers' Supply.

MUCK AGAIN!

'Well I've had my eyes tested and they'll let me know when they're ready. Is there owt else about me you think needs improving while I'm in the right mood?'

'One thing at a time. Anything of interest in Egremont?'

'Nowt that would interest you. There were some new milking buckets and a new brand of calf feed in the Supply but that's of little interest to you.'

'It is if you buy some, our buckets are so thin that you can very nearly see the milk inside. They're so badly bashed that they don't stand up level. It would be lovely to have a few new things for the cooling house. Remember that everything should be clean and hygienic, and that's very hard with buckets that we've had for years! Anyway, it's no good talking sense to you, sit down and have a snack before you go out to do the milking.'

'Oh! There is news from Egremont.'

'To interest me?'

'Aye, your May has got herself engaged.'

Edith sat down with a bump.

'Engaged? I would have thought that she'd have come and told us! Did you see her?'

'As well as I could without my new spectacles. She was outside the jeweller's looking at rings,'

'I must go and see her in the morning. There'll be all sorts of preparations to be made. I wonder if she'll be married here in Egremont or near his parish in Formby. Then there's all the dresses to buy! Esther will be surprised when she comes in.'

'So will the vicar if she's set her eyes on somebody else. Tom was saying that she's a very fine-looking woman.'

Edith stopped short in her tracks.

MUCK AGAIN!

'You mean Tom Graham knows she's getting married before I do? Did she tell you about it in front of Tom?'

'She's said nothing to me, she didn't even see me, but Tom could see what she was up to from the other side of the Main Street.'

Edith breathed a sigh of relief. 'It's a terrible thing Jackson when a respectable woman can't look in a shop window without half the town deciding that she's marrying again!'

A thought suddenly crossed her mind. 'Jackson, you didn't tell Tom about John? You didn't say she was seeing a vicar did you?'

Jackson smiled innocently and decided to string her along for a bit.

'What's wrong with telling the truth Edith, we have nothing to hide. Surely you're not ashamed of a vicar joining the family?'

'We'll be the laughing stock of the district!'

'How do you make that out? Are you ashamed of your sister marrying a vicar/'

'Of course I'm not, I'll be delighted if she marries such a lovely man, but if you've told Tom Graham all about the courtship ... and then there's no marriage, you won't dare show your face in the Grey Mare in case you're laughed out of the place.'

'I told Tom about her seeing somebody, but I never mentioned a vicar.'

'Thank God for that, but the idea of a marriage is very premature. It may come to nothing and you've put talk into people's mouths.'

'What's the gossip?' asked Esther as she came in from the yard.

MUCK AGAIN!

'Only your father busily telling Tom that your Aunt May is courting. Wait until she hears about it, she'll come storming into here to tell us to mind our own business.' Jackson's face lost its mischievous look as the thought washed over him. Life can become very complicated when you go to have your eyes tested.

'What made you mention it Dad?'

'She was standing outside the jeweller's on the Main Street. I saw her but she didn't see me. Tom said there were trays of rings on display, so I happened to mention that a chap was courting her, so she might be looking for an engagement ring.'

Esther's face beamed.

'I should think you're right Dad, what did Tom think about us having a vicar in the family?'

'He says he never mentioned that. I hope he didn't in case it all falls through then we'll be the laughing stock of the district.'

'Well, I think it's very exciting. I hope Dad's right. I can't wait until she comes. Is she too old to have a baby Mam?'

Jackson roared at the thought, his body shaking with merriment.

'Don't be so silly.'

'I don't know how old she is Mam. The whole thing is really romantic.'

'I can hardly trust your father to go to Egremont without spreading rumour and gossip throughout the district.'

'It was your idea that I should go, if you'd just left my eyesight alone you wouldn't have sleepless nights worrying about the local gossip or whether May traps a husband or not.'

MUCK AGAIN!

'Never mind Dad, judging by what you saw I think you're probably right. My goodness what will they say in the Grey Mare when they hear that you've a man of the cloth for a brother-in-law.

'That's no problem Lass, I'll just explain that these things are ... the will of God!'

16.

SOMETHING NEW

'What did you say that Dad bought in the auction yesterday Bill?'
'A donkey.'
'A what? Why do we need a donkey?'
'We don't, but apparently an old chap from Cleator Moor put one through the ring and no one gave a bid, so Dad decided that he'd help things along. I suppose he felt sorry for the chap! One or two bids were called, so seeing the interest he decided to push the price up a bit to help out, but of course the bids suddenly stopped and the donkey was knocked down to him!'
'He'll probably end up feeling a darned sight sorrier for himself than the old man, did he tell you all this?'
'No, it was Tom Graham. He let Dad out of his car, I could see him getting out as I walked down the road. Believe me I was very surprised when Tom stopped his car and told me about it. He wants us to know the truth and is curious about how Dad will explain things to us!' Esther chuckled.
' Have you any idea when the donkey is coming?'
'About four o'clock this afternoon.'
'Does Dad know anything about donkeys?'
'I have no idea, but I imagine he does, he's always handled horses and ponies, so he must have some knowledge.'
'What are we going to do with it? Wait until the likes of Alan Steel see it grazing in our fields! I have a feeling it

won't capture the imagination like the little Dexter cow did!'

'Anyhow Esther, we'll have a bit of fun at his expense at dinnertime, he must say something then or else the wagon will arrive and Mam is likely to have a heart attack with shock if he doesn't tell her!'

As the morning wore on Esther spoke to her father a number of times expecting him to say something, but he never uttered a word. He must be worried, she thought, or else he would have mentioned the addition to their stock. She couldn't help smiling to herself and trying to imagine how he would justify his new purchase.

At twelve o'clock both Esther and Bill hurried into the kitchen, not daring to look at each other in case their father became suspicious. Edith dished up a chicken pie and they all set to.

'Is can't be one of our chickens Edith, I haven't killed one for a good bit.'

'No, you're right, I bought it from Jack Brown's stall on the market, it's a lovely plump one.'

'So it should be, he wouldn't dare give you some old scrawny hen that's scratched around his yard for the last five years or so.'

'His hens never scratch about in the yard any more, he has one of those intensive care places.'

'You mean intensive breeding Mam, intensive care is in a hospital!' Chuckled Esther.

'Don't correct your mother Esther, it's all the same sort of thing. The care must be intensive if they never wander about feeding themselves and the farmer has to do it all. It isn't for me, I prefer the poultry to be self-supporting. I don't reckon they can do this intensive caring with ducks, they need plenty of water to splash about in …'

Esther took a quick look at Bill, but he was ignoring both her and the conversation. She was beginning to wonder if Tom had been wrong, if her father had bought the donkey then maybe he'd sold it later outside the ring. Her patience was being stretched to the limit, but her father was still decrying the modern methods of poultry keeping as though everything was normal. Then her ears picked up a change in his tack.

'Talking about animal welfare,' he was addressing his remarks to his children now, and they both took notice.

'I bet neither of you has noticed how Peggy's level of health has deteriorated since she foaled.'

'She looks as fit as she did before she had her foal, I was just thinking how a week or two's rest has made her look as good as she was before,' said Bill, puzzled by his father's remarks.

'I agree with Bill, I saw the foal gallop across the field and she trotted after her as if it was her first foal. I haven't noticed anything unhealthy about her, but you're far more experienced than we are Dad, so if you've noticed a change in her then you'll be right. Maybe she needs a few more weeks'' rest to spend with the foal.'

'No she doesn't need any more rest or else she'll take badly to being taken to work in the fields and leaving her foal behind, it'll be hard enough as it is.'

'Well, you have me worried Dad, how can we get her fit again?'

Jackson nodded.

'I've been thinking about this for a week or so now …'

Esther and Bill wondered what was coming next.

'Edith, you'll remember when every farm of any size used to keep a donkey . . .'

'I can't say I do,' said Edith vaguely trying to search in her memory.

Bill and Esther looked at one another and tried very hard to keep their faces straight.

'Oh, that's a very strange to keep Dad, why did they spend money buying a donkey that eats its head off and can't work for a living?' asked Esther innocently.

'That's where you're wrong Lass, every animal on an efficient farm has to earn its keep. A donkey certainly can. The old farmers used to swear that a donkey prevented Grass Fever and other conditions that affect horses. I bet you don't know that almost every racing stable has at least one donkey for the same reason. As well as for health reasons, race horses enjoy the company of a donkey and some of them won't go to a meeting unless the donkey goes as well.'

Esther and Bill were now stifling their giggles as best they could.

Edith was suddenly alarmed.

'Jackson ... surely you haven't ... you can't have ... bought a donkey?'

'A donkey?' echoed the two children in well-faked surprise.

'I'd been thinking about Peggy's loss of condition only yesterday morning, when a lone donkey was put through the ring.'

'And you were daft enough to bid for it? The last time you bought something we didn't need was Peggy herself, but at least she could work for her keep. I think it's about time I went to the auction with you, it's too dangerous to let you loose on your own.'

'I think it's a good idea,' said Esther wickedly, 'we have plenty of space and good grass, the poor little thing might have gone to be slaughtered for dog food or something.' Jackson felt cheered by such support.

'There you are Edith, you aren't looking at things in the right light. She is a bonny little thing.'

'What's her name Dad?'

'Jenny.'

'Why did her owner get rid of her? Can you count her ribs? Does she bite? Has she got any teeth to bite with?' snapped Edith.

Bill joined in with his questions.

'Did Tom see you buy Jenny?'

'Aye, he did, you should have seen his face? But he found a chap with a small trailer who's fetching her here.'

'When?' asked Edith.

'About four o'clock this afternoon.'

'What are you going to do with her? She's probably not used to sharing a field with cows and big horses.'

'Now, just leave things to me Edith. I'll put her into a hull and give her a bucket of water and a good feed when she come s. But after that she'll have to graze. It's bad for donkeys to overeat.'

'You seem to know something about donkeys Dad.'

'Like I've said before, all big stables had them and I spent a lot of time helping out in the stables of the local gentry. I saw a good few donkeys. There used to be little donkey carts that were used by the gardeners to cart stuff about a big estate.'

MUCK AGAIN!

'We haven't such a thing Jackson. If you want to set it to work you'll have to ride her. At least it won't be far to fall if you come off. Just think what the neighbours are going to say when they see a donkey trailing about with the cows. We'll be the laughing stock of the district!'

'Somehow I think Dad'll be able to deal with whatever they have to say,' laughed Bill.

As Esther workedduring the afternoon her thoughts kept returning to the little donkey, she hoped it would fit in with the rest of the farm animals and be happy with them. At teatime they were having a snack before they started the milking when a car with a trailer on the back drew into the yard. They all went out, apart from Edith, to look at the donkey. Ben as the chap was called opened the back of the trailer and led the donkey out into the yard then drove off. Esther was the first to stroke and pat the little animal. Jenny seemed quite happy to accept the fussing.

'She'll be used to pats and petting,' said Jackson, 'a donkey that's spent all her life on Cleator Moor will be used to children making a fuss of her.'

'I'll take her into that small hull near the byre where she can get used to hearing the farm noises? I'll feed her and give her a good brushing.'

Jackson nodded.

'Look out in case she gives you a kick, we don't know her yet. The brushing is a good idea, that'll soothe her and settle her down.'

'I can't see her hurting me if she does kick. Just look at the size of her feet, they are tiny!'

'Remember that daft Shetland!' warned Bill, she looked harmless but she could be wicked if you let your guard drop.'

MUCK AGAIN!

'Donkeys usually have a better temperament because they're a companion to their owner.'

'Why did the man sell her?'

'He was about to go and live with his daughter and she had no field, so he thought that the auction was probably the best place to sell her.'

'He was right, she's lovely. Tomorrow she could go into the paddock for the day, then when the cows go out there for the night after milking time she'll maybe feel that it's her field.'

'It depends on the cows,' said Bill doubtfully, 'you know what they're like, they'll probably chase her all round the place.'

'I'll keep an eye on her, and rescue her if need be.'

'Good Lass, we can think about putting her with the horses later. Peggy's the one that might object because of the foal.'

Later that evening as they sat by the fire discussing the donkey Edith interrupted them.'

'I notice that you're all talking about Jenny as though she's been here for years and none of you have mentioned giving Peggy's foal a name. She's a pedigree, so I'll have to enter her name on this application form from the Clydesdale Stud Book, so give me a few suggestions.'

Immediately they began to suggest names.'

'I think Bubbles would be a good name because she's always dashing about and kicking her legs.'

'That's no good Esther,' said Jackson horrified, 'they'll think she's a poodle. It has to be something very sensible for a heavy horse breed. The favourite names in the stud book are usually Scottish as it's a Scottish breed, Jean, Jennie and Peggy are favourites.'

MUCK AGAIN!

'We can't give her the same name as her mother or the donkey,' said Edith tartly.

'I know,' said Esther, 'If she should have a Scottish name let's call her ... Heather.'

They all looked at her in surprise.

'That's a super name,' said Bill, 'it suits her, what do you think Dad?'

Jackson smiled and nodded approval.

'We've never given a name to an animal so quickly. Heather will do fine, write it on the form along with the rest of her title Mother.'

Everybody was pleased about naming the foal, but Edith wasn't happy at all about keeping the little donkey that had already settled herself down on her straw bed.

*   *   *

Jackson knew what to expect as soon as he entered the Grey Mare a few days later.

Once he had settled himself close to the roaring fire a few of the regulars drew their chairs up near his table.

'Have you gone religious Jackson?' asked Harry Jepson.

Even Jackson was surprised by such a question.

'How do you make that out Harry?'

'Well, it's just coming up to Easter, so we were thinking that maybe you plan to ride up to the church on Easter Sunday on your new donkey. It's in keeping with the happenings of Holy Week.'

'Now that's not such a bad idea, but I don't reckon I'll have the little donkey cart ready by then. Edith wouldn't hear of me spoiling my best clothes by riding on a donkey. I bought her because she save me the cost of dosing my

182

horses, donkeys keep diseases away ... but I wouldn't expect you chaps to know anything about that.'

'How's she getting on with the rest of the stock?' asked Tom Graham hoping to direct the conversation into easier channels.'

'Fine, she's made friends with Heather, Peggy's foal, and she puts up with no end of nonsense from the daft little thing.'

'You'll have to go on holiday to Egypt if you want to sell her,' said Alan Steel, to the obvious enjoyment of the men gathered near the bar.

Jackson carried on laying his domino pieces before he replied.

'Egypt would be no good for her, she's being spoilt to death every day by Esther, then Edith and Bill. At first Edith wasn't sure about us having a donkey around the place, but ever since she spotted the cross that every donkey has across its shoulder, she's sure that Jenny's a sort of lucky charm. I don't think any of them would let me sell her now. So when your horses are sick, you needn't think of borrowing her because she's too popular to part with.'

'I've never heard of a donkey warding off disease!'

'How many have you kept Alan?'

'None.'

'Then you don't know anything about it. They say it's the donkey muck that gets into the soil and kills off some bacteria or other. The rest of the grazers benefit.'

'I all sounds a bit far-fetched to me,' said Joe Watson who'd been listening attentively, 'you're very good at pulling the wool over people's eyes.'

MUCK AGAIN!

Jackson laughed, 'some of you have the wool pulled over your eyes, and your minds, before I open my mouth.'
'Where did you learn all this then?'
'Those of you who put bets on the horses should be able to answer that.'
'Some of the drinkers from Egremont turned to hear the farmer's explanation.
'I can see that a few of you standing over there are regular punters on the horses.'
The men nodded and a few agreed enthusiastically.
'The next time any of you go for a day out to Carlisle races, just take a look round the back where the horse boxes are and you'll probably see a donkey or two tied up, some of them highly-strung race horses won't travel without their donkey friend.'
'I think I've heard about that,' said one chap who was leaning on the bar.
Tom who was seated in a dim corner watching and listening, thought about the bidding in the auction and marvelled at Jackson's ability to field the questions. Even he was almost persuaded that the buying had been deliberate. But Jackson had always been a good friend and he wasn't going to say what had happened, besides he was enjoying the repartee.
As the evening wore on the conversation changed directions a number of times as Jackson knew it would, but he was also aware that the presence of a donkey among his stock would provide the likes of Alan Steel with a fair amount of ammunition.
'Never mind' he thought to himself, 'the old donkey isn't likely to last until next Easter,' when he'd looked in her mouth there was hardly a decent tooth left.

MUCK AGAIN!

'We should have called her Methuselah,' he said softly to himself. 'Did you say something?' Asked Tom.
 'No not really, I was just thinking aloud.'

17.

CYCLING

'I wonder what time your father intends to arrive back home?'

Esther looked up from her magazine, 'what are you worried about? He'll be busy talking to somebody, you know what he's like. Farm sales are places where farmers see others that they haven't seen for years.'

'But he went on his bike.'

'So what are you worried about?'

'If he has one or two drinks too many then he could have an accident or even if he falls off he could be badly injured. He's not as young as he used to be. You young folks can fall off easily then get back on and you're no worse for wear but he can't.'

'Hasn't he gone with Mr Shepherd?'

'Yes he has, that's a good thing because he won't be on his own, but they are both late.'

'Mr Shepherd doesn't drink Mam, so he'll be in good company.'

'Yes, I suppose you're right, I shouldn't be so silly.'

'Just you settle down while I make us a cup of tea. Have you any cake in the tin?'

'What a daft question, there's always plenty of cake in the big tin.'

Edith immediately felt sorry that she'd snapped at Esther.

'Sorry,' she said, 'but I have a feeling that something's wrong.'

'Don't apologise, I understand.'

'It's such a long way to bike all the way to Gosforth and back. He should have asked Tom to take him in his car, I'm sure he would have taken them both.'

'At least we don't have to worry about the milking. Before we had a milking machine it was hard work doing the milking without him. We needed all the hands we could get. At least he won't be asking if we've finished all the cows, or did we water the bull!'

'No, that's one good thing about the new A.I. service. All the Shorthorn bulls we had were temperamental, I dreaded watching you or Bill leading one across the yard to the water trough. Plenty of farmers have been gored to death by bulls. It only takes a minute of carelessness and then it's too late.'

Esther returned with two mugs of tea and a slice of cake each.

She could see that her usually calm mother was very uneasy. But as the evening drew in there was still no sign of her father.

Esther was becoming anxious as well but tried to hide it from her mother.

'Should we ring the hospital, or the police?'

'If anything was seriously wrong the police would have called by now,' said Esther unconvincingly, 'perhaps one of them has had a puncture and you know how long that can take to repair. Or if neither of them has a repair kit they could be walking home.'

The words had hardly left her lips when they heard the sound of footsteps approaching the farmhouse door.

'Don't you dare tell him I was bothered about him Esther.'

MUCK AGAIN!

Esther laughed and nodded assent.

The back kitchen door opened and Jackson came through. Edith stared at her husband, he was standing soaked to the skin, water dripping all over the floor.

'Good God! What has happened to you? Esther, fetch your father a big towel while I bring him a clean set of clothes, he'd better change here in the back kitchen or we'll all be soaked. Then you can tell us what on earth has happened to you.'

Twenty minutes or so later all three were seated close to the fire with mugs of hot tea to hand.

'Tell us how you came to be so wet Jackson, then I'll make you a hot supper.'

Jackson began his tale.

'The sale went well and we each bought a few handy implements as we always do at a farm sale, it's the last thing we can do for a good friend. Ernest bought a scythe and I managed to pick up a couple of bridles cheaply. Then we set off home. Ernest had a job to tie the scythe to his back but we managed it.'

'What a dangerous thing to have tied to your back when you are riding a bike.'

'Aye, it is Edith, but by God it was hard work trying to ride up the hill out of Gosforth, we had to get off and walk up it, after that all the hills slowed us down. We soon discovered that we can't do what we used to.'

'You should have had the sense to set off earlier, I hope you didn't have a few pints?'

'Just a couple earlier in the day, but Ernest Shepherd doesn't drink or else I would have had a few more, so we can't blame that for what happened. But I'm starving

MUCK AGAIN!

Edith go and put the frying pan on then I can tell you about it in comfort.'

He turned to Esther, 'have you done the milking and seen to the stock?'

'Yes, there were no problems. The milking machine does all the work now so there's never any need to bother about coming home late. But you put the wind up Mam, she was worried to death. She was convinced that you'd had an accident.'

Soon they all three of them were enjoying plates of bacon, eggs, black pudding and mushrooms.

Once they'd finished and the dishes were washed Jackson continued his account.

'As we turned off the main road at the Iron Bridge it was starting to get dark and the lamps on our bikes weren't so good, but we knew the way, so off we went down that long hill towards Kersey Bridge. Ernest had already said that his brakes weren't so good, but we hadn't had any problems up till then because the hills hadn't been so steep and long. My brakes were good so I took my time down the hill. You know how it goes on forever?'

Esther nodded.

'Ernest had disappeared into the darkness ahead and I was so scared of riding into the back of him that I slowed down. At last I reached the bridge, there was no sign of Ernest. I thought he'd have got off his bike and waited for me. As I slowed down to cross the bridge I was sure that I heard a cry so I got off the bike and looked over the parapet. The cry came again.

'Help! I can't get out of the water, I'm drowning! Jackson! Jackson! Can you hear me?'

'It was Ernest?'

MUCK AGAIN!

'Aye, it was, I could scarcely see him, but I shouted down for him to keep calm, I was coming. As you know the beck is deep under the bridge and if he was caught in something he might well drown. Then I remembered the scythe tied to his back! I had visions of him cutting himself to pieces!'

'Good God!' Edith gasped, 'you must have been terrified and you could have been drowned yourself!'

'When these things happen you don't see the danger, you just wade in, which is what I did. I scrambled down to the edge of the water and I could see him tangled up in his bike and somehow stuck fast. I knew I had to get him out of the water.'

'And you can't swim!'

'That's right, as I waded into the deeper water I could feel my feet lifting off the bottom. I was bothered in case I was swept away from him downstream. But I made a big effort and managed to grasp his bike, so then the bike was holding us both and keeping us from being swept away. I was bothered in case he was injured. He said his arm was injured but he didn't know how bad.'

'What about the scythe?'

'Believe it or not it was till tied firmly to his back but I had to be careful not to cut myself as I pulled him towards the bank. At that point a car drove over the bridge, we both shouted but quickly realised that we could neither be heard nor seen, we were too close to the bridge.'

'Oh My God!' gasped Edith, 'thank God you're safe! How were you saved?'

'Let Dad tell us.'

MUCK AGAIN!

MUCK AGAIN!

'I could see that Ernest was shocked and beginning to lose consciousness, and he was so low in the water that the waves washed over his face and he had to splutter and cough to keep breathing. I pulled and pulled to try and get his legs free of the bicycle frame.'

'But what if his leg was broken? It must have been very painful for him.'

'Aye, I thought about that, but you have to do something quickly, so I decided that it was better to be alive with a very bad leg, than to be dead with a leg that I'd kept as good as it could be. Anyhow, I just desperately tugged him and his scythe from the frame. I knew he was unconscious by now and couldn't feel any pain if I was hurting him. By now my own legs and fingers were pretty numb but I wrenched and pulled in sheer desperation. Believe me Edith, I prayed like mad as. At last I pulled him free and dragged him to the bank. He was starting to moan so I knew that at least he was breathing. Looking up I knew I had little chance of pulling him up to the road, but I'd have to give it a try. I began to drag him inch by inch from the edge of the water. Then I heard the sound of a motor car coming down the hill towards the bridge, so I scrambled up and stood in the middle of the road and waved my arms in the air.'

'Thank God!' said Edith, 'but you could have been knocked down in the dark!'

'I was aware of that, but thank goodness they saw me and stopped. Two men were inside and they jumped out asking what I was doing standing in the middle of the road in the dark. But as soon as I explained they carried Ernest up the bank and put him in their car.'

'What's happened to him Dad, is he still alive?'

MUCK AGAIN!

'The chaps said they'd take him straight to the hospital.'
'What about you? Didn't they offer to run you home?'
'Aye, they did, but I wanted Ernest to be seen to, because I thought that he was in danger of dying. I told them that I lived close by and would rather cycle home.'
'I wonder if Mary Shepherd has been told, she must be worried to death.'
'I should think the police will inform her of the accident, they usually do.'
'I could put my coat on and go and tell her.'
'No Mam, it's a good three miles from here and you don't know what to say, you don't know how badly injured he is. Leave it to the authorities. We'll hear how he is in the morning.'
'Esther's right Edith. I've done as much as can, so leave it to the doctors.'
'You know what Dad?'
'What?'
'You saved Mr Shepherd's life!'
'Don't talk daft, I just helped him a bit.'

*   *   *

'I see you're in the papers again Jackson!' laughed Tom Graham as he stopped his tractor at the field gate where the old farmer was looking at his herd of milking cows that he'd just driven into the field.
'You've hit the headlines once with your triplets and again when you pulled Ernest Shepherd out of the beck.'
'The headlines?'
'Aye, you should see today's Whitehaven News you're a hero.'
'Does it say how Ernest is?'

MUCK AGAIN!

'Aye, he has a broken arm and plenty of cuts and bruises, he told the reporter that you saved his life.'

'I did what I could Tom, it could have gone either of us. It's at moments like that, that you realise that nature is much stronger than we are and it's just a case of luck whether we win the battle or not.'

'You sound serious, don't get too miserable or you'll never give us a good laugh again.'

'No chance of that, a fright like that one makes me realise that our lives can be whipped away in a few short seconds. So I intend to enjoy what's left of it as best I can.'

'Are you going back home now, I hear there might be a newspaper reporter or two coming to interview you.'

'No, I'm off down Anchor Lonning to check the stock down there. If you go back past our house and you see any of them, tell them to go and talk to the two lads in the car who were the real heroes, I doubt that Ernest could have survived much longer if they hadn't arrived on the scene.'

As he walked down the lonning he reflected on the events at the bridge. Maybe Edith was right about prayers, he had prayed so hard for help – and it had come. He would be sure to put a bit extra on the collection plate when he went to church on Easter Day. Christmas and Easter were the only times he went, he'd always left that side of things to Edith, she had the knack of finding the right words.

He thought about the talk recently about putting men on the moon, surely the scientists were putting the cart before the horse?

They should get the bicycle right first!'

18.

MODERN MUCK

'**A**s Jackson rode along perched on the front of his cart he leisurely viewed the countryside with the farming activities going on in his neighbours fields. Peggy sensed the lack of urgency, let her mind wander. Now that her foal was growing up she was less anxious about returning early to feed her. Anyway, the new strange sort of horse that had come to live on the farm recently had made friends with the foal and they happily played in the field together. Besides, she could now graze a little so she was never as hungry as before. Peggy shook her head sadly, the world of horses seemed to be changing. She was used to meeting friends as she walked along the road, and stopping to have a friendly nuzzle, but apart from Captain who lived at home, she rarely met other horses nowadays. Occasionally they met some that were ridden by their masters but they weren't her kind, they never seemed to have time to stand and chat, they danced and snorted as if they were a superior breed to her.

She looked forward to seeing her foal when she reached home, but foals were changing too. She used to gallop after them, but now she felt this foal was deliberately mischievous and delighted in galloping at full tilt when there was really no good reason for doing so. However, she noticed that the strange sort of horse called Jenny couldn't keep up with the foal either so it wasn't just her. Peggy had heard her master calling her foal 'Heather' and she wondered what the name meant, perhaps it meant … naughty.

As they were now going along at such a slow pace she reached over and pulled a mouthful of grass from the dyke then paused for a moment before chewing it to see if her master was angry, but no, he didn't seem to have noticed! Yes, times were definitely changing. She was pleased because a slower pace of life was very welcome. She eyed the forbidden grass ahead and debated whether she dared snatch another mouthful … life was suddenly becoming fun!

Jackson was busy with his own thoughts. For the first time in his life he was looking at his neighbours closely. The sound of tractors and farm machinery drifted across the countryside. He was one of the few left who was working with horses. Perhaps he was hiding his head in the sand? Like many farmers' sons Bill was working at Sellafield and Esther was thinking about applying for a job there. He could understand them, the work was easier and cleaner and the wages were high. Good pensions were on offer, and he knew that if he'd been a young man he would have been tempted.

In the factory there were plenty of folks of their own age. It was a young factory with a young, clever workforce, he hadn't anything better to offer.

He also reckoned that he wasn't too old to learn to drive a tractor, after all, some of the men he could see driving them across the fields had fewer brains than the horses they had once worked, so no doubt he would manage. With a tractor … and maybe one of them fancy milking parlours he could do the farm work with little help. He chuckled to himself as he imagined what the family would say if they knew the way his mind was working. The chap who'd demonstrated the milking parlour had said that there were some grants going, so he reckoned it was about time that he got something for nothing! Edith had been talking this way for a while now and maybe she was right. If they'd owned the farm it might have been a different story. Suddenly he felt a bump as a wheel touched the hedge. That damned sneaky horse! I daren't take my eyes off her for a minute. 'Come on, move along … and earn your keep!' he said to the surprised animal.

Maybe a tractor would be more obedient? He looked along the horse's back as she walked briskly along, the sound of her hooves beating a sharp tattoo in his ears. Yes, she was only flesh and blood, it was time for her and Captain to do the lighter work. A tractor could pull uphill faster and could be left to stand without wandering off to eat forbidden grass.

What about the cows? A milking parlour! That would take a bit more handling, his cows were spoilt and temperamental and would need a lot of persuasion. Still, it would be a challenge. He decided to keep his decisions to himself for a while, such a sweeping change would have to be handled with sensitivity and diplomacy, slower brains would have to be informed with delicacy and tact.

*   *   *

'You've what?' asked Edith thunderstruck, 'you've ordered a tractor?'

Jackson nodded, his eyes twinkling as he reached for another slice of bread.

'Yes, I've decided that we must move with the times. I wouldn't have it said that I'm not a forward looking farmer.'

'Well, that makes a change! I thought modern machinery would never find a place on this farm! Why the sudden change?

'Now Edith, you've made the mistake most women make about their husbands'

'And that is?'

'You're very sure that you know what we're thinking! But often that's a mistake because if we have any intelligence at all we are able to think about things and weigh them up. It's necessary, if we're to make progre ss, to change our plans according to the world situation and the national economy.'

'Don't say you've been reading one of those financial newspapers somewhere?'

'Where on earth would I read a financial paper? They don't have them in the Grey Mare. No Edith, I've been thinking things out and I've decided that I don't want to be left behind in the farming world.'

'Have you any particular sort of tractor in mind?'

'One of them Ferguson's would do me nicely. I've looked at one in Cockermouth and I found it easier to climb onto than scrambling into our cart with that daft Captain dancing about.'

'I'm not so sure about it Jackson, I seem to remember the last time you thought about buying a tractor you had problems stopping it, it was lucky you aimed for a hay stack.'

MUCK AGAIN!

'Trust you to look on the down side. I once learned how to drive horses and they have wills of their own, I reckon that with a bit of help I'll be fine.'

'What about the money to pay for it?'

'We're not doing too badly now and I'm told we'll get a grant for the milking parlour.'

'The milking parlour?' echoed Edith. 'You intend to buy a milking parlour as well?'

'What's the use of half measures when we modernise? It'll make my work a lot easier now that Bill isn't working here full time.'

'What will the neighbours say?' gasped Edith as she sat down on the nearest chair.

'What have they to do with my farm? I don't tell them what to do with theirs. Besides, I like to keep folks guessing. I wouldn't have told you, but I thought you might think unusual was going on when the chaps come to dig up the yard for the new milking parlour.'

Edith was glad she was sitting down.

'Now Edith, I don't want you to say a word about all this. I want to keep the neighbours guessing as long as possible. The tractor will be delivered at the end of the month so Bill can have a go driving it, he says he can drive a tractor.'

Jackson chuckled to himself as he watched Edith's face recovering from the shock.

'What will happen if the electricity supply fails?'

'I thought I was the old-fashioned person in this house. I'll have to milk them myself of course.'

Edith sat for a few minutes absorbing what her husband had said then went on uneasily.

'What will Bill and Esther say when they come in?'

MUCK AGAIN!

'They're not paying for the new machinery and as far as I can see they won't be using it as much as I will.'

Edith began to laugh, things were taking a definite turn either upwards or downwards. They'd had difficult times in the early days so a change now could be no worse and the children could fend for themselves now.

'Yes, we can take risks now Jackson. Looking back folks always said that 'where there's muck there's money' but we've had plenty of muck but precious little money!' Jackson nodded.

'That's true, but more than likely we had the wrong sort. Maybe what we need is the oil and grease sort of muck!'